MY LAUGH-OUT-LOUD LIFE:

THE
DASTARDLY
DUO

BURHANA ISLAM

Published by Knights Of
Knights Of Ltd, Registered Offices: 119 Marylebone Road, London, NW1 5PU

www.knightsof.media
First published 2022
001

Written by Burhana Islam
Text and cover copyright © Burhana Islam, 2021
Cover art by © Farah Kahndaker, 2021
All rights reserved
The moral right of the author and illustrator has been asserted

Set in Bembo std/ 12 pt
Typeset design by Marssaié Jordan
Typeset by Marssaié Jordan
Printed and bound in the UK

A CIP catalogue record for this book will be available from the British Library

ISBN: 9781913311285

2 4 6 8 10 9 7 5 3 1

MY LAUGH-OUT-LOUD LIFE:

THE
DASTARDLY
DUO

BURHANA ISLAM

For Sméagol,
I couldn't have done this without you.

~~HIGHLY CLASSIFIED~~
~~FOR YOUR EYES ONLY~~

By Agent Yusuf Ali Khan (Age: almost 10)

This is NOT a diary. I repeat: THIS IS NOT A DIARY. This right here (what you're reading right now) is the legacy of Yusuf Ali Khan: the first, the last, and the one and only... ME.

You see, when Affa got married and left to go live in Manchester without us (yeah, I know. She actually left ME of all people — it's a good thing that I trained to survive without her), well, she made me promise to put the zombie book she gave me to some good use. If you know Affa, then you'd know that she can be very persuasive. Affa said that if I recorded my missions in this top-secret V.I.B (Very Important Business, obviously) file, then she'd make it worth my while. We all know what that means: HELLOOOOOO KRISPY FRIED CHICKEN WINGS, flaming hot popcorn bites, chips coated with delicious, mouth-watering goodness, and a purple Fruit Shoot. Nanu always says to never make a deal with the devil, but sometimes Affa can just be so TEMPTING!

So here it is: Agent Khan's (that's me) highly classified detective file. Here you'll find ENEMY NUMBER #1, the 5B Re-vengers (like the Avengers, but cooler), and a foiled plot to take over the world (AKA our city, AKA our school, okay - AKA maybe just our WHOLE, ENTIRE CLASS). Like I said, this is serious business. Only open if you dare...

CHAPTER 1

"And then," I whispered, making sure that all the grown-ups had left the snack room, leaving us entirely alone, "It got worse."

Aadam nibbled on his chicken wing in fear, as Saleem tried to hide behind him. He had one hand on Aadam's shoulder and the other covering his eyes.

"Maybe you should stop now, Yusuf," Mustafa squeaked. He buried his head in his dashiki shirt and trembled.

But I carried on, now hissing. "The whole place was covered in a thick oil of complete darkness." They were all in a trance. MY trance. Who knew I wielded such power? Thor's hammer, come at me! "Then, when the clock struck midnight, there was a snap, crackle and POP that got louder and louder and louder... but nobody knew where it came from."

"What was it?" Saleem shrieked, pulling his hair. "What happened?"

Mustafa's teeth were chattering and Aadam was now nibbling on his nails! But Sairah rolled her eyes. Well then, I'd have to kick it up a notch.

"Then there was silence. Complete silence." I locked eyes with Sairah. Even though she and Saleem were twins, they had nothing in common. Scaring her wasn't easy. "But all of a sudden, under the ghostly light of the moon, HE DEEP FRIED HIS OWN MEATY LEGS!" I gasped, waving my fingers in the air for dramatic effect.

"Say it's not so, Yusuf!" Aadam shrieked, jumping from his seat. "Say it's-"

But Sairah rudely interrupted him. Talk about a tough crowd. "I asked for frightening stories, not fried chicken stories!"

"Shhhhh! I'm trying to listen," Mustafa said, waving her down. "And then what happened?"

"We are NOT listening to another story about a deep-fried goose!" Sairah stomped her feet and took another bite out of a Krunchy Chicken wing (they were nothing on Colonel Krispy, trust me).

"Oh, well if that's the case, I don't have any other scary stories." I scratched my head and searched my brain. "Unless you count Nanu coming into my room last night?" Nanu had asked me which sari would be best for today's Hajj reunion party. I shuddered at the memory of Nanu's fashion show.

"Something tells me that's about to change," Saleem was pointing to the door that Bashir was about to walk through.

2

We all groaned. Only the 5B bully was capable of spoiling our fun. He wasn't called Bashir the Basher for nothing. The five of us huddled closer together, pretending not to notice him. We had to protect our plate of food at all costs.

"I'll be back in a second, Ammu-jan." Bashir called over his shoulder. Rumour had it that he had mastered the art of being deceptively nice the day he was born. He had almost everybody at the mosque fooled. Everybody except us (and God, of course)…

Slowly, Bashir closed the door and turned the blinds, trapping us all in. Whatever his cunning plans were, he had made sure that there'd be no witnesses. Only a mastermind villain would think like that. When Bashir finally turned towards us, he had the most evil of smiles etched into his face. Saleem whimpered and shuffled further behind us. Trust Saleem to use ME as a human shield. Didn't he know that I needed protection too? I was nothing without my HULK SMASH HANDS!

Bashir paused. He rolled his sleeves and cracked his knuckles.

This was not good.

CODE RED! I repeat: this was NOT GOOD!

I clenched my fists to stop them shaking.

Saleem was right.

We didn't need a scary story.

We were in one!

GULP!

CHAPTER 2

"Yusuf Smelly Khan," Bashir sneered. "We meet again." He eyed me up like a lion sniffing a meerkat, but instead of laser scanning me and the others, his eyes snapped right to the last chicken wing.

It was one thing to threaten me, but to threaten my munchies? "Not on my watch, you don't." I slipped past Sairah and swiped the crispy goodness from its resting place. I shook the little wing in his direction and wiped that smile right off Bashir's face. Batboy mode: successfully activated.

"You go, Yusuf!" Aadam cheered, clapping his hands. "You eat that wing. You show him who's boss." I could almost always count on Aadam to have my back. He was my favourite cousin after all.

"You snooze, you lose." Mustafa laughed, turning to high-five Saleem. Bashir death-stared Mustafa down until his smile disappeared from his face.

Even though I was trying to be Captain America confident, my belly was like jelly. It was definitely a sign to fill it once and for all. Just as I was about to nibble on my mouth-watering prize, it was stolen from my very hands!

"If you're not fast, you're last!" Bashir shook the wing and almost popped it into his mouth, but my supersonic speedy skills were always ready to save the day.

The wing was now back in my possession, even if half of its crust had fallen to the floor. "Better learn to be quick, Bashir. If you don't eat fast, you don't eat at all. MUHUHUHAHAHA!" Oh, wait! Did I say that last bit out loud? Did I have a death wish?

Bashir's eyebrows twitched.

I had definitely said that last bit out loud!

Bashir lunged at the chicken, trying to tear it from my grip. "It's mine!" he hissed. "I haven't had one. Stop being so greedy."

Me? Greedy? Was he for real? We had a whole room of snacks and he went for MY CHICKEN WING! If that wasn't greed, I didn't know what was.

Sairah and the others backed off, leaving me and the Basher in an invisible arena to fight to the death (or at least until the chicken was gobbled up).

"It was on my plate and I've already licked it!" I pulled harder.

"Just give it to me, Yusuf!" Bashir tugged and tugged, but no way was I letting go. Sweat was trickling down my palms. I couldn't be sure if it was mine or Bashir's. The little wing didn't stand a chance. It was already crumbling all over us. If you listened closely, you could even hear it crack.

"It's not worth it," squealed Saleem. "It's probably got the lurgies from being touched all over!"

"Shush, Saleem!" Aadam called. They seemed so far away. Safe. "It's probably even juicier now."

I didn't want to admit it, but Bashir's death-grip was stronger than mine and the wing was nearly touching his lips.

"PULL!" Mustafa shouted.

But I couldn't. He was too powerful, and my shoulders were starting to ache. I wouldn't be able to hold on much longer, but I didn't want to look like the loser either.

"Have it your way, then." I stammered, trying to catch my breath. I counted to three before letting go.

But that was absolutely, catastrophically, completely the WORST DECISION I had ever made.

Bashir the Basher went flying into the snack table and crash-landed on the floor. Cupcakes and cheesecakes tumbled all over him. To top it off, the chicken wing that had been launched into the air fell **SPLAT** on Bashir's forehead.

I froze.

Silence completely swamped the snack room. Nothing could be heard except our heavy breathing. I was too scared to look too closely, but one thing was certain: Bashir the Basher lay lifeless on the floor. Worst still, it was all my fault.

CHAPTER THREE

"Poke him," Mustafa whispered. "Just check he's not dead."

Bashir hadn't moved for 53.2 seconds and neither had we.

"I'm too young and handsome for prison!" Aadam wailed, throwing his hands in the air, and collapsing against the wall. "I'm not going to survive there!"

"Shush! Let me think! Let me think!" My eyes darted to Bashir's splattered body.

"You're a dead man, Yusuf." Sairah said, shaking her head. "Why do you always get us into trouble?"

WHAT? "NO, I DON'T!" That wasn't fair. "If anything…" Oh wait – was she right?

"Guys, it's moving." Saleem whispered, pointing at Bashir's feet. "Look, his toes are wiggling."

"Should we throw something at him?" Sariah asked. "Or is that too risky?"

Before I could answer, a lone Jaffa cake soared skywards into the air. Aadam stared at it in sheer horror, realising his mistake.

"NOOOOOOOOOOOOO!" I yelled, stumbling

towards it. "Not the Jaffa cake! Anything but the Jaffa cake!"

But it was too late. The chocolate-slathered biscuit launched itself right into Bashir's open mouth.

CHOMP CHOMP!

"He's ALIVE!" Saleem screamed. "Run for your lives! He's alive!"

Everything happened at once.

Bashir pounced to his feet

armed with chips in one hand and samosas in the other.

Mustafa's voice boomed through the madness "TAKE COVER!" He dove under a table. "Save yourselves! Save yourselves!"

Aadam and Sairah grabbed their weapons: onion bhaji bombs, chickpea bullets and plummeting pakoras - they were both spicy and deadly.

And there I was, frozen in fear and centre target, waiting for everything to detonate.

"Well, well, well," Bashir said. His eyes glittered as the poison darts of the samosas were aimed directly at me. "What do we have here?"

With a heavy SWOOSH, Bashir shot his chips onto our turf, attacking us with potato arrows. Samosas blasted their way through the air, missing me by millimetres.

Then, above the chaos, the call for war was made. I tried to balance myself, and ignore the ringing in my ears as somebody yelled:

"FOOD FIGHT!"

CHAPTER FOUR

I watched from the safety of the table legs, snatching every lamb kofta ball, every jalebi and every curly fry that rolled my way. Nanu always said never to waste food, so I stuffed them in my mouth for safe-keeping.

Trying my best to stay hidden, I peered from under the table. Aadam was wobbling to his feet after slipping on a rasmalai. Mustafa was pelting Maltesers at anybody and everybody while Saleem hopped dangerously on one foot, trying to catch every little chocolate ball in his mouth. Thank God he was sticking to the five-second rule.

"Where are the grown-ups?" I shouted, but nobody was listening to me.

Pizza slices soared across the sky. The chocolate fountain gushed like Willy Wonka's waterfall all over the floor, and a bloody handprint (tomato ketchup, maybe?) stained the window. Nobody would be leaving alive.

OH NO!
"SALEEEEEEEM,"

I screamed. "What have they done to you?"

Saleem was flat on the floor and covered in ~~blood~~ sriracha sauce. His right hand was raised like he was going towards the light. "I'm dying," he cried. "Please tell my ammu that I loved her biryani."

"Don't go! Don't touch the light!" I searched frantically for Aadam and Mustafa. Surely they could save him?!

"Yusuf!" Sairah screamed, as she karate chopped the Nutella cupcakes attacking her.

Quicksilver had nothing on Sairah Miah.  "Where are you? I can't hold on much longer!"

Sairah was right. Her arms were flapping in all sorts of directions, but her lightning-speed was starting to slow down.

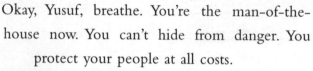

Okay, Yusuf, breathe. You're the man-of-the-house now. You can't hide from danger. You protect your people at all costs.

SLAP! Suddenly, I tumbled to my knees, squirming in pain as the grandfather of all spring rolls flew into my stomach.

"Man down," I yelled, gasping for breath and clutching my tummy. I tried to straighten my glasses and steady myself to see the culprit of this heinous crime.

And there he was: Enemy Number #1, grinning like only Thanos could. Bashir the Basher. He bolted to the snack table for ammunition.

"NOOOOOOOOOOOOOOO!" I shouted. Affa always said to stand up for myself and make sure that my voice was heard.

Well, Bashir the Bashir, you'll be hearing me from NOW ON!

"FOR AFFA!" I yelled, swiping a Nutella cupcake and launching it across the snack room at full force. "TAKE THAT!"

But Bashir ducked and dodged it, letting the cake go flying SMACK onto the Imam's white thobe.

My heart stopped. It just stopped. I was dead.

AAAARRRRRGGGGHHHHHH! FOR THE LOVE OF JAFFA CAKES, when did the most important person in the whole entire mosque get here? Where was he when I needed him? I hadn't thrown anything this entire time!

The Imam locked eyes on me. Inna lillahi wa inna ilayhi rajeeon (we say this when we lose something, remember? Like a human being or an iPad). I'm a dead man. DEAD, I AM.

"Enough," Ustadh Saleh shouted. He was both our mosque teacher and the mu'adthin (the caller to prayer), and he had the voice of a HUGE HERD OF ANGRY ELEPHANTS.

At that moment, silence ripped through the chaos. The only sound that could be heard was the plopping of the chocolate cupcake, as it slid off the Imam's thobe and onto the cold, hard floor.

CHAPTER FIVE

Think of the scariest thing you can imagine. Then times your fear by 6.8 million. That was how we were feeling.

We were all lined up like criminals, facing the front and shaking. There was a pizza slice stuck to the ceiling, jollof rice scattered everywhere, and chicken tikka masala bleeding on the walls. Our audience was scarier than the police, much scarier than a top secret super-spy agency, and even scarier than Affa after she found out that I had ruined her wedding dress two days before her big day. Yes, you

guessed right. It was our grown-ups, staring in horror into all of our souls. Something told me that middle names would be involved.

"How dare you?" Ustadh Saleh began, pacing up and down the line. He was careful to avoid the flattened gulab jamuns and profiteroles in his path.

I don't know who looked more ashamed: us or them. Trying not to scan the line-up for Amma or Nanu, I stared at my feet. It was risky business too since so much sweat was sliding off my nose! I didn't like this at all. Not one little bit.

"How dare you come to a HAJJ reunion party," Ustadh Saleh continued. "A gathering all about how we should continue to improve our character, about how we should strive towards goodness, a gathering about community and unity! - HOW DARE YOU ACT LIKE A BUNCH OF WILD CIRCUS ANIMALS?" He rounded his head like a python and hissed. (I think a zoo would have been more accurate, but now wasn't the time to correct him.) "Wallahi, God as my witness, you have five seconds to confess your crimes or you will feel my wrath." He said the last three words really slowly, and each one was like a punch to the throat.

"My Bashir would never do anything like this." Obviously, Bashir's mum would think like that. She wouldn't see dirt even if it was stabbing her in the eyes. "Isn't that right, baba?"

Baba?

BABA!

That made me SICK! There was nothing baba-like about Bashir! That was like saying a giant flesh-eating dragonoid-spider was really a newborn kitten.

"Yes, Ammu-jan." Bashir squeaked. "I was just minding my own business, doing absolutely nothing wrong when it happened. It was so scary!" He rubbed his eyes, PRETENDING TO CRY. Nobody would ever fall for that! There was absolutely no way on planet Earth, the Sun, the stars and the galaxies beyond, that anybody would ever fall for that.

"My poor boy!" Bashir's mum squealed.

Never mind.

"Come to Ammu-jan!" she said, patting her own eyes dry. "Let's go before they upset you even more, baba. Let me treat you to Krispy Fried Chicken."

ARE YOU KIDDING ME!?

Aadam even felt brave enough to almost roll his eyes, but Khala was eyeing him like a hawk. Both she and the Imam folded their arms.

With a swoop of her abaya, Bashir the Basher and his mum escaped from the clutches of Ustadh Saleh without a scratch.

Only God could help us now because, like it or not, we were next…

CHAPTER SIX

"Sairah Rahma Miah," the Imam said. "Do you have something to say?" He tried to rub off the chocolate stain with his hands, but it just looked more and more like a number two every time he tried.

Of course the Imam would start off with the class detective. Sairah knew everything about everybody, and everyone knew it. MI5 and the FBI had nothing on her. Sairah tugged the bottom of her black dress and started chewing on her jumper. She only ever did that when she was plotting and scheming ON HOW TO WORM HER WAY OUT OF TROUBLE! She was an expert at that. Only she could run the school's secret newspaper 'THE 5B TIMES' and get away with it. To this day, the teachers had no idea that she was the culprit reporting on all the classes' crimes.

After Sairah shook her head seven times, it was Saleem's turn. I held my breath, as his eyes turned googly and he flopped to his knees.

"I was just trying to eat the food," Saleem cried.

His hair bounced wildly every time he shook his head. "I didn't want to waste any of it." He crawled to his amma, grabbing the bottom of her skirt in desperation. "You have to believe me, Ammu! Say you believe me!"

If I had the guts to do that, Amma would pretend she didn't know me. There'd be no way his mum would fall for that. Something in my stomach told me that things weren't going to end well for us.

Mustafa was next in line, then Aadam and then me. Even though they were my best friends, Mustafa and Aadam were the WORST sidekicks to have your back. All Mustafa's mum had to do was blink at him and all his secrets would spill out. She was already giving him the stink-eye; it was a miracle he hadn't cracked already.

"I'm just going to take the twins, and erm… go, if that's alright with everyone." Without another word, Sairah, Saleem and their amma swooped out of the room, which left me, Aadam and Mustafa in the firing line.

Dear God,

Please don't let Mustafa be next. Please. I'm begging You. I'll do anything. ANYTHING!

"Mustafa."

Oh man!

Ustadh Saleh walked right up to him and stopped just in front of his nose.

"Ahem," Mrs Jallow said, straightening the ruffles on her dress. "Let me handle this, please."

HANDLE THIS? That could only mean one thing! I stared at Aadam in sheer terror. My eyes darted to Amma and Nanu. Khala was glaring at us too. Don't do it. Don't make eye contact. Confess now, Yusuf, before it's too late!

Just as I was about to spill the beans, Mustafa's mum stepped forward.

"Well?" Mrs Jallow said to Mustafa, crossing her arms and tutting. She wasn't screaming in the slightest, but she may as well have been, the way her tuts were echoing in the silence. "I brought you into this world, boy. You don't think I can take you back out?"

Mustafa's bottom lip trembled and SO DID MINE! There was definitely an earthquake on the move!

"You better have something to say in the next five seconds, Mustafa Jallow, or I'll be sending your backside back to Gambia. You hear me?"

And before anybody could even count to one, Mustafa crumbled, dropping me and Aadam in it.

CHAPTER SEVEN

"Me mam told us EVERYTHING," Liam said. We were at school, the day after The Incident. Miss Minchell had just run into the Year 6 class, so he was being extra brave by swinging on two legs of the chair. He was pointing at me, while Saleem whispered something to Sairah. Everyone was eyeing me suspiciously. I even had to double, triple check that I didn't have any snot hanging down from my nose (all clear - Alhamdullilah).

"Told you what?"

"She heard from the next-door neighbour who heard from the lady at number 20 who heard from the man at the end of the road whose friends with the people at the mosque that YOU, Yusuf Ali Khan, are an almost-murderer."

"AN ALMOST-WHAT NOW?"

The whole class gasped and shushed, as Sairah whipped out a pen and notepad.

"I told you," Saleem muttered, putting down his reading book. "He just can't control himself."

My cheeks burned. "No, I'm not!" I snapped. At least FOUR PEOPLE here had witnessed the showdown yesterday. Why was nobody clearing my name? Amma and Khala had already banned Aadam from the house as punishment. Why was I suffering more?

"The whole street was talking about the Hajj party," Liam continued. "And how you threw a rock at the Imam."

"WHAT?" A ROCK?

"I heard it was a brick," Bashir added.

"And how you knocked him clean out," Liam continued.

"What are you saying?" I spluttered. WHAT WAS HE SAYING?!

"And how you stuffed cheese-string in his mouth to silence him." Saleem squealed.

"A cheesy P.E. sock, not a cheese string. Get your facts right." Sairah was scribbling so quickly that her pen was almost smoking.

'GET YOUR FACTS RIGHT?'

DID SHE REALLY SAY THAT?

"You were there!" I spluttered. This was a nightmare. I hadn't woken up yet. Yeah, that was the only reasonable

27

explanation.

Liam piped in again. "Me mam said that if the Imam hadn't been rushed to hospital right there and then, then he would have died and you would have been sentenced to death!"

Mustafa's jaw fell open. "Yusuf, you didn't tell me that happened!" He moved his chair away from me. **CREAK, CREAK, CREAK.**

"You were there!" I said, shaking my fists. "Stop making things up, Liam. You don't even know what an 'Imam' is! Maybe we should call you Lying Liam instead." 'Lying Liam?' You go, Yusuf! Funny and savage. What more could I have asked for? Hopefully, that would be enough to clear my name.

"Yeah, Lying Liam, why lie for?" Mustafa said, pointing at his chest. Where was that energy before?

"My mum said you've brought shame onto your family," Sairah said, swinging her pen my way.

I shook my head. NO WAY!

Bashir nodded. "Yeah, I heard my khala say that your ammu-jan will always be known as the mum of the boy who threw a boiling hot chicken curry at the Imam. She won't be able to walk down the street anymore without being shamed."

"Shamed?" My family? MY OWN FAMILY? NO!

This could not be happening! Not Amma and Nanu and Affa. Well, okay, maybe Affa, but not Amma and Nanu! "YOU WERE THERE!" I shouted. Why was the truth being buried in this huge WEB OF LIES? "I threw a cupcake at you, Bashir – nobody else, but YOU!"

"So you admit it?" Saleem squeaked from behind his sister. "You tried to kill the Imam. Your poor ammu. She unknowingly made a murderer.."

"I know," Sairah agreed. "Your family honour has gone down the drain, Yusuf, and it's all your fault." Sairah paused. "So how do you feel about these accusations? Are you going to confess? Are you, are you, are you? Just tell us you did it and we'll go easy on you."

Mustafa shook his head. "Man, you should have told me."

"You were both there!" I shouted, almost pulling out my hair. "You saw everything!"

"I didn't see nothing," she finished, snapping her notepad shut. "Justice will be served."

Before I could try and make sense of this madness, Miss Minchell slipped back into the classroom with a HUGE BOX of mysteries.

"Well, 5B," she said, smiling widely. "Have I got a surprise for you!"

CHAPTER EIGHT

"A Form Captain!" Miss Minchell said, tapping her pen on the table. Her brown hair wiggled, and her left eye twitched every time she got excited. She was twitching so much that if she was a robot, she definitely would've exploded. "Responsibility like that doesn't come easily.

It's not a job for the faint-hearted." Her eyes passed over Saleem, who tried to wriggle back into his school jumper. "No, not at all," she continued slowly. "The Form Captain will hold a seat on the prestigious school council, be a voice for the class, and represent 5B when making very important decisions for the school."

Only God and Miss Minchell knew what 'prestigious' meant, but it sounded so COOOOOOL. Imagine having that much power and that was without the help of a HULK SMASH HAND. I WANT IT. I WANT IT ALL!

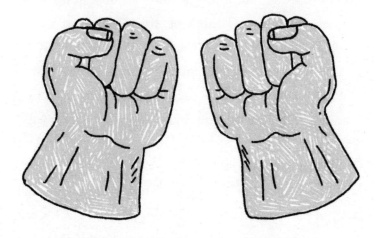

Mustafa kicked me under the table (ouch!). "Are you thinking what I'm thinking?"

"SHHHH!" Miss Minchell said. "Otherwise, you'll be here at break-time."

We both sat up, silent.

"To be Form Captain, you'll have to be a leader, you'll have to have a way with words, and you'll have to inspire change for the better." Miss scanned the classroom like she was looking for a hero in the rubble.

"I'm right here!" I wanted to shout, but I didn't just in case she gave me jail time at dinner. I couldn't afford to sharpen pencils today. I sat up even straighter and folded my arms. I kept a finger to my lips and looked directly at Miss. But everybody else was doing the same thing! Sairah had even put a pen behind her ear to look more serious. Why didn't I think of that? I only had a glue stick. This battle for Form Captain would not be easy.

"We'll be holding elections in three weeks." Miss got out of her chair and paced the classroom. "In that time, those of you who are brave enough to run need a campaign."

"What's a campaign?" Bashir asked.

"Sorry," Miss said, putting her hands over her eyes like a set of binoculars to scour the room. "I thought I heard someone, but I didn't see a hand up so I MUST HAVE imagined it."

SHOW TIME!

I shot a hand up in the air.

"Yusuf?"

Yes!

"Miss, please, I wanted to ask what a 'campaign' was if you could so kindly answer. And please can you tell me how much pain this involves. Please." I smiled with all my teeth and Miss almost tripped backwards. I sometimes had that effect on people. Hold the smile, hold it, hold it.

Bashir was furious at my good manners. Mission accomplished.

"Watch and learn," I mouthed.

"Ahem," Miss began. "Not camp-PAIN, but a 'campaign' is when you organise something to show people that you're the best person for a job. You can make posters persuading people to vote for you, talk to the class to convince them you're the right person for the job, and deliver a speech." She nodded and sat back down. "In three weeks, we'll have ballots, special voting slips and pens. It's a really honourable position and when you go to secondary school, you can tell your teachers that you were a leader."

WAIT ONE SMELLY SECOND! Did Miss just say 'HONOUR'?

LIGHT BULB MOMENT #1

CHAPTER NINE

"You saw what Bashir did at the end of the lesson," Mustafa said at break-time. He opened up a packet of popcorn and passed me and Aadam a few. "He'll never let you run for Form Captain, not if he has anything to do with it."

Mustafa was right. After Miss had delivered her speech, she had asked the class if anyone wanted to try out for Form Captain. Everybody put their hands up and I mean EVERYBODY, even Saleem. But Bashir death-stared everyone into forfeiting - everyone except me, anyway. I had some serious honour to regain, and no amount of eyeball wars could change that.

"Oh man," Aadam said, picking a popcorn kernel from between his teeth. "And he made you look like a complete loser with no honour, no brain and no sign of intelligence at all."

I scratched my head and took another popcorn. "I don't think he did that."

"Yeah, he did." Mustafa nodded. "Look, he's doing it now."

In the corner of the yard, Liam and Bashir were running around in circles shouting

"SHAME ON YOU! SHAME ON YOU! SH-SH-SH-SH-SH-SH-SH-SH-SHAME ON YOU!" The bees in my stomach were buzzing.

Even Sairah and Saleem were staring at them from the far wall, waving a sheet of paper like a flag.

"We need to take him down," I said through gritted teeth. "We need a plan."

Mustafa stuffed his popcorn in his pocket and licked his lips. "We need to make the best Form Captain campaign the world has ever seen and make you sound so amazing that you'll have to win."

"Good idea."

"Or," Aadam added. "We could sabotage Bashir's plan, get revenge for the Hajj party and then annihilate him."

"Better idea." I nodded. "I'm in. We could be the 5B Re-Vengers, avenging the class crimes!"

"Hey, what's wrong with my plan?" Mustafa looked up, raising his eyebrows.

"We need to be prepared." Aadam said, jumping on the spot. "Bashir and Liam are going to rig the votes. Word on the streets is that he's stolen Miss Minchell's red marking pen and he's going to change any votes that aren't for him."

"No way!"

"Yes way," Aadam nodded seriously.

Mustafa grabbed my arm. "I found this in his drawer." He pulled out a card with a joker on it.

"You went into his drawer!" Was that a brave move or a bad move?

"Desperate times call for drastic measures, remember?" He passed me the card. It was old and creased.

"Woah." Aadam inspected it. "You know what this means, don't you?"

I shook my head. Something wasn't right.

"It means he's going to make a deal with the Masked Trickster," Mustafa finished. "And that we're in big trouble if he does."

"The who?"

"Don't you know?" Aadam asked.

I shook my head. Maybe all signs of intelligence had left my body after all.

"The Masked Trickster is a real-life legend." Aadam waved his hands, huddling us closer together. "He's been responsible for the biggest school pranks in human history."

Oh, man. The bees in my stomach were back again. I hadn't even noticed that they'd gone.

"Yeah," Mustafa said. He lowered his voice, making my ears prickle. "He once placed a whoopie cushion on the headteacher's chair in the Year 6 Leavers Assembly."

"You're joking!" He had to be joking, right? Nobody on earth would be foolish enough to do that.

"He once let off a stink bomb when Mr Boakye was in the teacher toilets." Aadam smiled like a wild animal. "Some of the Year 1s almost lost their lives because the fart cloud was so nuclear."

This wasn't good. Not. At. All.

"Yeah," Mustafa continued. "Then one day, the trickster did the mother of all pranks."

I bit my nails. THIS was the criminal Bashir had on his side? What chance did I stand?

"It was a dark, stormy Parents Evening and all the lights in the hall were out." Mustafa began to whisper. "All the teachers were quiet, preparing their papers and things, and when they finally went into the hall, **BAM!**"

I jumped and knocked into Aadam. He was so pale that he looked almost a little bit like Liam. Now that was scary.

"The hall was covered in wet toilet roll, flour bombs and rotten, stinky eggs." Mustafa plugged his nose. "That was the last anyone ever saw of the Masked Trickster. After that, he vanished without a trace."

"Woah," I said, finally taking a breath.

"Yeah, I know." Aadam said.

"You don't stand a chance, mate." Mustafa pulled something out of his pockets. "Especially not after this." He handed me the goods.

It was The 5B Times and it read:

THE
5B TIMES

BASHIR THE BASHER:
BEATING HIS WAY TO VICTORY!

THE FATE OF YEAR 5 RESTS IN
THE HANDS OF BASHIR THE BASHER OR
YUSUF ALMOST-MURDERER KHAN!

CHAPTER TEN

"HOW COULD YOU DO THIS?" I stormed
up to Sairah and pushed the 5B Times into her hands.
"'THE FATE OF YEAR 5 RESTS IN THE HANDS
OF BASHIR THE BASHER OR YUSUF ALMOST-
MURDERER KHAN'?!" I already knew the article off
by heart.

Had she lost the plot? WAS THE PLOT ACTUALLY
LOST?

"Stop shouting at me," Sairah said firmly, crossing
her arms like SHE HADN'T RUINED MY ENTIRE
CHANCES OF REGAINING MY HONOUR!

"I AM NOT SHOUTING AT YOU!"
I shouted back. She crossed her eyebrows and stomped
her feet. Sometimes she reminded me of Affa, a very
angry Affa. "I'M SHOUTING AT SALEEM!"

Saleem took two steps back like I was the enemy – me,
of all people! Couldn't he see that his sister was ruining
my whole life? Where was the justice?

"You need to calm down, Yusuf Ali Khan." I hated to admit it, but she was right. Mr Boakye was patrolling the playground, and his head was turned in our direction. WHY WAS SHE ALWAYS RIGHT?

I tried to breathe... breathe... BREATHEEEEE slowly. "Is what you've written true?" I snatched back the 5B Times. Please say no, please say no, please say no.

"It's the news," she twisted the tails in her hair. "Of course it's not true...."

Phew!

"Yet," she finished.

"What?"

"She said 'Of course it's not true... yet.'" Saleem nodded, peeling his banana.

"I HEARD WHAT SHE SAID!"

"Why did you ask?" For a 'shy' boy, Saleem was feeling veeeeerrrrrrry confident right now.

"Look, you need to calm down and turn around." Sairah pointed at Bashir and Liam, who had started circling one of the Year 4s. The poor kid didn't stand a chance. He was clinging onto his cheese for dear life. He should have surrendered his Babybel when they first asked. FOOL BOY ERROR. "When you look at Bashir," Sairah continued. "What do you see?"

I adjusted my glasses and zoomed in. Bashir had gone

into fist-mode and Liam was hovering behind him. "I see a mean, big bully, who's a liar-liar-pants-on-fire and a nasty-pasty. He's actually worse than Thanos and that's saying something."

"That's exactly what I see." Sairah quickly crumpled up the newspaper and almost took a bite, pretending it was an apple just as Mr Boakye passed us. His superpower was stealth. If we weren't careful, we'd pay for it.

Saleem nodded again. "He's gone. We're in the safe zone."

"What do you mean that's 'exactly' what you see?" What planet did Sairah live on? I took the paper off her and uncrumpled it. "Bashir the Basher is THE FUTURE of 5B." I read. "He's an inspirational leader, a smooth-talker and a pioneer for change. There's no denying it. With him in charge, 5B will always get what they want."

"Which part of that don't you like?" Sairah said, taking the paper back and scanning it again.

ARE YOU KIDDING ME?

"Which part of this is on my side?" I had to stop myself from pulling my hair out and scratch my arms instead. Little flakes tumbled to the ground. "Sairah, because of you, I'm falling to pieces. LITERALLY! Look at me!" If she wasn't careful, I'd turn into a cheese pasty before her very eyes (you try living with eczema - it's not easy, I tell you).

Sairah turned to Saleem, who was making his banana skin into a boat. "Saleem?"

"Isn't it obvious?" Saleem asked. "It's spy-speak, Agent Khan. Learn to decode. Bashir ALWAYS inspires me to hide. He's definitely a pioneer for change too. One time he changed the colour of my skin by giving me a bruise, AND he ALWAYS gets away with it. If he's not a smooth-talker, I don't know who is." Saleem nodded. "So I'm voting for him. Sorry, Yusuf, but you don't stand a chance."

CHAPTER ELEVEN

Okay, so my plan to interrogate and intimidate Sairah and Saleem wasn't working as well as I had hoped. I thought they would've fallen to their knees by now and begged for my forgiveness, but it turned out, just this once, that I may have been a teeny-weenie, incy-wincy, tiny-whiney bit wrong.

It was time to get the big guns out.

"Look," I began. This would be my juiciest deal yet. Something so clever, so irresistible and so tempting that there would be absolutely no way on planet Earth, the Sun, the stars and the galaxies beyond that Sairah Rahma Miah could even utter the word no. "If The 5B Times is on my side, I'll make it worth your while." I teased. "I'll give you ALL the inside scoop on the student council first. You'll know everything before everyone else does."

"NO WAY!" Sairah's eyes got bigger.

"YES WAY!" I knew that would be an offer she couldn't refuse!

Saleem laughed.

What was so funny?

"NO WAY are you bonkers enough to believe that I can't get the inside scoop myself. Yusuf, do you even know that you're in the presence of a mastermind journalist?" Sairah rolled her eyes. "Thanks, but no thanks."

Wait, what?

"You're not interested?" Oh man. I thought I'd clinched the deal with that one. "But what about working for the greater good? We need to team up and expose Bashir for the criminal he is. There's no way Miss Minchell will let him run for Captain if she knew. Do you not care about justice?"

Sairah twisted the pen in her hair. "Yusuf, Yusuf, Yusuf." She put her arm around my shoulder.

WHY WAS SHE TOUCHING ME? GET AWAY GET AWAY GET AWAY. ARGH! I helplessly watched her fingers near my neck. I just hoped Aadam and Mustafa didn't see this!

"I do care about justice, but only when it's just us." She pointed at Saleem and her belly button. "This is why you'll never ever, not even in a million years, become Form Captain."

"What do you mean I'll never be Form Captain?"

"She means that good people never make it to power," Saleem piped in, licking his banana peel. "So, like I said before, you don't stand a chance."

"What if I made it more interesting?"

Sairah looked up. "I'm listening..."

"If you help me win, I'll smuggle you a pack of Oreos."

"Now you're speaking my language," she smiled. "Make it two and you have yourself a deal."

"Let's meet in the middle and say three packs," I said. Future leaders had to be great negotiators.

"You've got yourself a deal!"

BOOOOOOOOYAH! BOOM SHAKA-LAKA-LAKA! BOOM!

As I walked away, feeling like a MIGHTY MEERKAT, I heard Saleem squeak to Sairah, "That's the person you want leading 5B?"

Yes, Saleem Miah. YES INDEED!

CHAPTER TWELVE

Something wasn't right. This definitely wasn't here beforehand.

I was in Affa's room, unpacking my schoolbag. Even though Affa didn't live here anymore, Amma still kept her room as HER ROOM. It was almost like a museum and even her cheesy socks and used tissues (GROSS) were exactly where she'd left them. (they probably even still tasted like Whotsits too - don't ask). When Affa wasn't here, and she rarely ever was, I liked to use her room as my top-secret, undercover den, and this was exactly the place where I discovered THE THREAT.

The message was loud and clear. Somebody had cut out the headlines of newspaper clippings and stuck them on a sheet of paper, before stuffing it in my backpack.. If you looked closely at the edges, you could almost see specks of blood (or chili sauce, of course I licked it to see). If they wanted to scare me, well, IT WAS WORKING!

It had to be Bashir the Basher or Liam. There was no way anybody else would have the guts to take on an

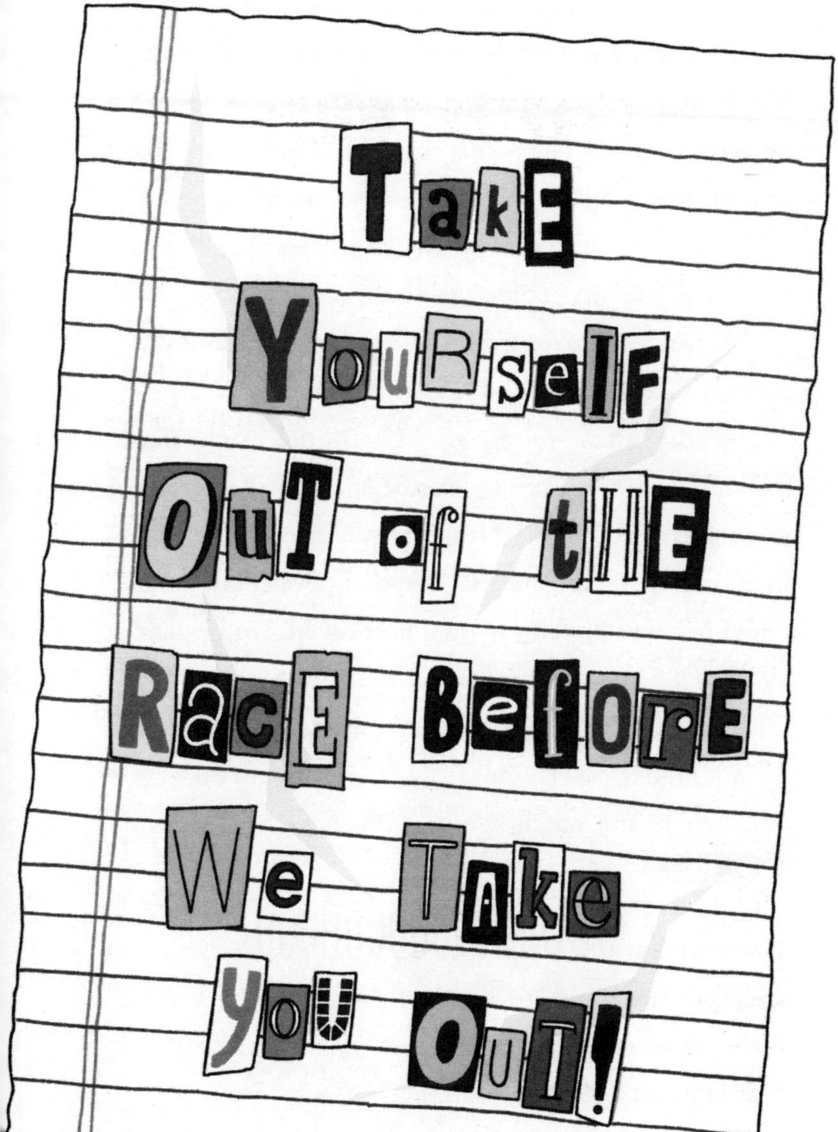
TAKE YOURSELF OUT OF THE RACE BEFORE WE TAKE YOU OUT!

almost-murderer like me. Unless… that was what the culprit wanted me to think. For all I knew, it could be Sairah and Saleem. Those two probably had so many copies of The 5B Times that they could probably make a million notes and swim in them. They were supposed to be on my side, but these days, when you were on the path to power, you just couldn't trust anybody.

"It's just a joke, Yusuf," I said to myself. "Nobody will actually take you out. You hear me? Nobody."

Outside Affa's room, the clock tick tick ticked LOUDLY almost like my heartbeat. I had no choice but to go into stealth mode. Nowhere was safe now, not when lives were being threatened. They (whoever THEY were) could have infiltrated my own home. I had to be alert at all costs for my own health and safety. But what would I do when they finally trapped me? I needed to get wisdom from a higher power, especially when my enemies were everywhere and watching my every move…

CREAK!

"NAAAAAANNNNUUUUUUUU!" I

shrieked. "Save me!"

"Yes, Eesoof?"

ARRRRGGGGGHHHH!

"Nanu!" I held my chest tightly, where my heart was

trying to lunge itself outside of my ribcage. "When did you get here?"

"Well, it all started when my very own Nana and Nanu-jan got married in a little fisherman's village by..."

Not again.

"I mean, when did you come into my top secret... Affa's room?" I interrupted her. Nanu couldn't know about my underground lair. There was no time to waste with lives at stake - my life mainly.

"Oh," Nanu pressed the tasbeeh (her prayer beads AKA strangulation weapon) in her hands. "I came about ten minutes before you started licking your Affa's cheesy socks."

"You saw that!" I stared at her in horror before remembering to keep my cool. "I mean, I wasn't licking them, just sniffing them. I'm not that gross."

Nanu raised an eyebrow.

"Annnnnnnywayyyyyyy..."

"Ji, beta?" She put the goggles that were her glasses on Affa's pillow and squinted hard.

"I need your help."

CHAPTER THIRTEEN

"So you see, Nanu," I explained to her, while tapping her fingers one by one so she stayed awake. "If I don't become Form Captain, then I'll live a life of shame. Amma will always be known as the monster who raised a murderer and you'll always be known as the most evilest Nanu in the whole entire galaxy. We need our honour back ASAP. You see my dilemma, don't you?"

Nanu didn't say anything. She just kept staring at me.

"Erm, Nanu. Did you hear what I said?" Please don't say she fell asleep again.

"Don't move, beta." Nanu's hands searched silently for something. Her finger crawled over her walking stick.

GULP.

"Er, Nanu?"

But she wasn't listening. Instead her hand slipped into AFFA'S USED TISSUE BOX! Oh no! NANUUUUUUUUU NOOOOOOOOOOOO! There were centuries and centuries worth of snots in there. We would die. We would die! Nanu's little body wouldn't be able to fight… but wait. What was happening?

Nanu's fingers crawled further and further away from the box and closer and closer to the WORLD'S WORST WEAPON OF MASS DESTRUCTION: her slipper!

HOLY JAFFA CAKES! What was she going to do? Was SHE the enemy? Did she write the note? No, that couldn't be. Could it? No, Nanu couldn't write English. She never has. OR MAYBE THAT WAS WHAT SHE WANTED ME TO THINK! What did Nanu have to gain? SAY IT'S NOT SO!

I tried to reach for Affa's blanket so I could use it as a protective Captain America shield, but Nanu didn't take her eyes off me. Instead, she raised the slipper just above my head and FROZE.

"Don't move," she whispered.

Wait, what?

THWACK!

Nanu's slipper
smashed against
the wall.
It was
a good
thing I had
ducked otherwise
I would have seriously
lost my life.

"What was that for?" I yelled, gasping for air. I had only just managed to steady myself, but my heart had **ZOOOOOOMED** into the deep unknown…

"I was trying to hurt your honour," she said, getting out her little tin of gwa-fan and sliding a bite into her mouth. **CHOMP CHOMP.**

It was official: Nanu had lost the plot.

"You can't just hurt honour like that, Nanu. You can't hit something that doesn't actually exist!"

Nanu had been alive for almost a century. She was born WAYYYYY before Sheikh Google existed. How did she not know this?

"Are you telling me that honour isn't a real thing, my kholja tookra?" she scratched her head and put her tasbeeh back over her neck.

"Of course, it isn't!" Now back to business. "So, how do I get it back?"

"Listen, beta." Nanu tried to tap my fingers this time, but because she didn't have her glasses on, she was just poking my elbow instead. "This honour that you believe so much in, don't put so much weight on it. People will always talk. It's a fact of life, so stop focusing on what you can't control and focus on what you can control." Nanu brought her nose close to mine and touched it.

When two family noses connect, it's a noo-noo. It's

NOO-NOOS LAW. Look it up.

She stared at me with bulging eyes. "You want to be a good leader? You want to regain, as you say, your 'honour'?"

I nodded. "Sir, yes, sir!"

"Then show them through your character. Show them that you're more than the rumours they have spread. Show them what you're really made of. All you have to do is look after this." She pointed to my tummy and rested her hand there. "And if it makes you feel better, our family honour went down the pan before you were born. Your Abbu… ahem. I mean, don't fear the people, beta. Show them what true leadership looks like."

As usual, Nanu was 2,000,000.89% right. I took her glasses from the pillow and placed them on top of her nose so she could see clearly again. I should really go to a higher power more often. It was clear: if I wanted to be the best Form Captain ever, I needed to look after people's stomachs. The only way I could do that was with Amma's special CHICKEN SAMOSAS!

Miss Minchell's digestive system, here I come!

CHAPTER FOURTEEN

Every Tuesday, Wednesday and Thursday after school, Amma and Nanu always drop me off at the mosque. It's there that Ustadh Saleh closes the gate and traps us all in for two hours of his terrifying reign. His kingdom (AKA the mosque) is quite small and smells like old shoes.

At the mosque, we actually do a lot of important learning and, even though I'll never ever admit this to anybody else, it's actually quite fun. Especially on a Thursday because, if I sit at the very back, I can have a good nap after a long almost-week at school.

I snuck Aadam and Mustafa a Jaffa cake each and filled them in on everything.

"If you're bribing Miss, then I'll be in charge of the posters," Aadam announced, TOO LOUDLY. "Dad got me a new laptop, so I can make them extra special."

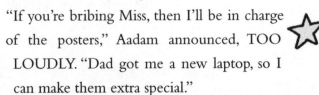

Ustadh Saleh gave us the stink-eye, so we had to put our heads down again. He was busy listening to Bashir read Qur'an at the front. Almost everybody knew that the 5B Basher was a big, bad bully, but when he read Arabic, somehow, he sounded exactly like Zain Bhika, an angel, and the snap, crackle and pop of Rice Krispies with cold milk on a hot summer morning all rolled into one. Between you and me, I was actually a little jealous.

"Leave the Masked Trickster to me," Mustafa whispered, when the coast was clear. "I'm going to try and make contact before Bashir does. With the ultimate prankster on our side, there's no way we'll lose."

"Good thinking." I nodded, pretending to turn my page of the book we'd been given. Ustadh Saleh's eyebrows were twitching. That was not a good sign.

"Don't worry about it, Yusuf." Aadam said. "I promise that the whole school will be plastered with your evil smile **MUHUHUHAHAHA!** If that doesn't make them vote for you, only God knows what will."

"SHHHHHHH! You're going to get us caught." Mustafa hissed.

I quickly ducked. Mustafa was right. Ustadh Saleh had now moved onto Saleem, but the ever-watching mighty eye of the mu'adthin hovered dangerously in our direction once again. He folded his arms tightly. We had to be more careful. Now was not the time to lose our Jaffa cakes. Who knows what kind of chaos that would unleash?

"Take some tapalapa with you, Mustafa. It might help." Aadam nodded seriously. "And ask your mum if she can save me some with that red sauce, please. In the meantime, I'm going to tell Sairah that Bashir and Liam have the worst lurgies in human history. I mean, even their lurgies have lurgies. YUCK! That should put everybody off." He shuddered at the thought.

Nobody, and I mean nobody, ever wanted to be an informant for The 5B Times. But, as always, desperate times called for drastic measures. That would have to be a risk we'd be willing to take.

"BOYS!" Ustadh Saleh shrieked, making the three of us scream ARRRRRGHHHHHHH all at once.

Was he trying to give us a heart-attack?

Oh great, now three million pairs of eyeballs were glaring at us. Why was it that when you needed a cloak of invisibility the most, it was absolutely NOWHERE to be seen.

"I've just about had enough of your antics! Talking during a Qur'an lesson? Have you no shame?" He waved

his pen like it was a spear. If he wasn't careful, he'd take somebody's limbs out. "Nobody has forgotten about the fiasco at the reunion last week. You three have a lot of making up to do! Next week's test should help you."

HELP US?! HELP US?!

"But, Ustadh," I wailed, "How exactly will a test help us?! It will do the absolute opposite of helping!"

"Yeah, remember what you said last week?" Mustafa piped in. "Testing is haram, sir. Only Allah can test us."

Ustadh Saleh's eyeballs looked like they'd explode.

Mustafa must have taken the hint because he said. "Only joking! Please don't tell my mum. Please. Please?"

Ustadh ignored him and turned to Aadam. "It's your turn. To the front, now."

"God help you," I whispered. A little du'a (prayer) goes a LONNNNNNG way sometimes.

"Ameen, brother," Mustafa agreed, covering his ears.

"Don't worry," Aadam winked. "I've been practicing all weekend. I'm going to NAIL it!"

If Aadam meant that he'd sound like sharp nails on a fresh chalkboard, then yes, yes he did. He absolutely NAILED it!

CHAPTER FIFTEEN

DAY ONE of OPERATION TAKE OVER THE WORLD (AKA our school, AKA our class):

"No way!" Mustafa yelled the next morning at school. He was reading The 5B Times and jumping up and down. "Tell me you're joking, Sairah. Tell me you're joking!"

My stomach had somehow plopped to my feet. I didn't know why exactly, but something told me that this was not good news. NOT GOOD NEWS AT ALL.

"Would I ever lie?" Sairah asked simply, twisting a pen in her hands.

"That's a trick question, right?" I took my coat off and put it on the peg, while sneaking my secret weapon into my pocket. Sometimes it was hard to tell if Sairah was being serious or not.

The whole entire class was BUZZING. Every single person had a copy of the newspaper. There was no escaping it.

"IT'S TRUE." Liam called, waving copies in the air. "IT'S ALL TRUE. ROLL UP, ROLL UP AND READ

THE EXCLUSIVE INTERVIEW OF OUR HERO
AND FORM CAPTAIN, BASHIR!"

WHAT THE ACTUAL FUDGECAKES?

I swiped The 5B Times off Sairah and read quickly.

ARE YOU KIDDING ME!? As if anybody on planet
Earth, the Sun, the stars and the galaxies beyond would fall
for this. You could smell the stinky lies from a million miles
away. Nobody, and I mean nobody, would take this seriously.

"I'm voting for Bashir!" Mustafa squeaked.

"Wait, wait?"

"More golden time, no Maths, extra P.E.,
cake for dinnertime. What's not to like?"
Mustafa read greedily. "An hour for break-

time too. Finally, somebody put their foot down!"

I gave Mustafa (THE WORST SECOND BEST FRIEND IN THE WHOLE ENTIRE WORLD) the stink-eye. I was getting pretty good at it now. "That's it. You asked for it. You brought this on yourself." I wiggled my packed-lunch box as a threat. "No more Jaffa cakes for YOU!"

Everybody gasped and there was silence. Just in time too, because Miss slipped into the classroom and The 5B

Times all melted out of sight.

"Did you mean that?" Mustafa whispered, while Miss did the register. "Are you really not going to feed me any more snacks?"

"You said you were voting for Bashir! He's arch-enemy Number #1," I hissed. "Here, Miss" I called out, just as she said my name.

"I'm your friend. Why would I do that?" Mustafa opened the dictionary and pretended to read it. This was not the time to tell him that it was upside down. "My mum always says sometimes people say things they don't mean. Like me voting for Bashir and you and the Jaffa cakes. I was just joking anyway."

"I didn't find it very f…," but my voice disappeared because Saleem had rolled me a note while Miss had her head down.

This was suspicious. Very suspicious. Saleem wouldn't risk his life to pass a note unless it was very urgent. I uncrumpled it and made out the scrawly writing. Saleem hadn't got his pen license yet.

'IMPORTANT. MUST READ. HIGHLY CLASSIFIED.

Our sauces tell us that there's a plot today to take you out'

GULP.

CHAPTER SIXTEEN

"Psst," Mustafa whispered. "Liam said that Saleem said that Sairah said to turn it over."

Honestly, between you and me, I wasn't ready for what would be waiting for me on the other side. When people talked about 'the other side', IT WAS NEVER GOOD!

Slowly, by the huge **THUMPING** of my heart and the JUMPING of my feet, I turned the paper over. Let me tell you that it wasn't easy work with sweaty fingers.

I read it carefully: 'of the presidential race.'

Wait, what?

I had to read it all together, so it actually made sense.

IMPORTANT. MUST READ. HIGHLY CLASSIFIED. Our sauces tell us that there's a plot today to take you out

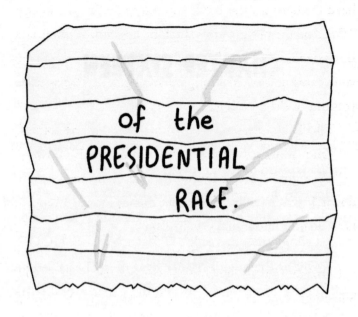

of the
PRESIDENTIAL
RACE.

Ohhhhhhh, that makes more sense. I mean, OHHHHHH NOOOOOOO! The sauces had decided my fate!

"Who would do something like this?" I whispered to myself.

"It's Bashir," Mustafa said, pointing to him and Liam. They were pretending to be good by correcting their spellings from yesterday.

"Obviously!" I hissed.

"Then why did you ask?" Mustafa crinkled his nose and turned the page of his upside-down dictionary. "Never mind. Anyway, I should tell you," he ducked his head further into the book and whispered more quietly. "Word on the playground is that the Dastardly Duo (that's Bashir and Liam, by the way) are planning to sabotage your campaign by making you so angry that Miss takes you out of the running."

"The 'Dastardly Duo'? How do you even know this?"

"I'm reading a dictionary, duh. I'm on the Rs now."

"Oh right." I didn't know Mustafa could read upside down. It was actually a lot harder than it looked. "I mean, how do you know that's their plan?"

"It says so in The 5B Times."

I groaned. Sairah's newspaper was the source of all evil. She might not have realised it yet, but it really caused more trouble than it was worth.

"Mr Jallow," Miss Minchell called, making both of us jump. She was ticking a piece of paper. "Can you come here, please?"

Mustafa closed his dictionary, put it on the table and took a deep breath. "Coming reluctantly…"

CHAPTER SEVENTEEN

Breathe, Yusuf. Breathe.

Breathe in... and breathe out.
In...
Out...
In.
Out.
Now shake it all about - no! You don't have time for this, Yusuf. Focus!

"I can do this," I said it to myself like a du'a.

Yep, I can do this. I can definitely do this.

The whole class was busy cutting and sticking worksheets in their books before the break-time bell. Sairah had already finished and was probably scribbling more ideas for trouble, TROUBLE, TROUBLE in her notepad. Saleem was sniffing his glue, while Liam was whispering something into Bashir's ear. Bashir had stuck his sheet at the back of the book, not the front and was now trying to peel it off without ripping the entire thing.

And Mustafa? Well Mustafa was chillin' like homemade chicken kebabs. He was busy colouring in. Miss said we could only do that IF we had done everything she had asked us to do.

But I WASN'T DOING ANY OF THAT. Why? Because Liam (who was obviously trying to be the shaytaan in human form today) had given me LEFT-HANDED scissors instead of right. He knew I was right-handed. EVERYBODY in this whole entire class knew I was right-handed. Last year, I even did my show and tell on my RIGHT-HAND because of how important it is! My left hand only had ONE JOB and this one just didn't cut it. LITERALLY!

ARGGHHH! I can't do this! What did I do to deserve this?!

"A'oodhu billahi min-nash shaythaanir-rajeem, a'oodhu billahi min-nash shaythaanir-rajeem," I had to keep saying it to get out of this nightmare. AND IT WAS A REAL-LIFE NIGHTMARE!

My work was already a mess because SOMEBODY (guess who?) mixed up all the pen lids. I had accidentally written in green ink instead of red. Then, I had to cross it out and cut wonkily a piece of blank paper to stick it over the mistake

(Miss doesn't let us use tip-ex because last time Bashir tried to blind Saleem with it). But then the glue stick went missing and was NOWHERE TO BE SEEN. Worse still, Mustafa had given his back and everybody on my table was finished except me. And to top it all off, it was break-time in about six minutes and I still was nowhere near finishing! WHY ME? WHY ME, YA RABB? WHY MEEEEE?

"Five second warning, Year 5," Miss Minchell called out.

FIVE SECONDS! What was I meant to do in five second with no glue, no scissors and no –

"Okay, time's up. Pens down."

. "But Miss!" That wasn't fair. She didn't even count it out loud. Where was the warning? It was called a five second warning for a reason, right? RIGHT?

Why wasn't she sticking to the unspoken rules? If you give a warning, you say it out loud! How else will your people be warned! Make this make sense!

"Yusuf! This is the third time today that you've not followed instructions." Miss clicked her fingers. Not the click! I wasn't made to cope with the click! "One more peep out of you and you'll be here at break."

In the corner of the classroom, Bashir and Liam were smiling. They had both folded their arms and put a finger to their lips. Surely, Miss would see right into their evil souls, right? RIGHT?!

Keep calm. Keep calm. Keep calm.

"Psssst," Mustafa whispered when Miss had turned back to the board. "It's time to get the big guns out. Your secret weapon."

Oh yes!

BOOOOOOOOYAH!

We'll see who's smiling then, oh Dastardly Duo. We'll see who's smiling then...

CHAPTER EIGHTEEN

"Ahem, Miss," I cleared my throat and put my hand up.

But nobody paid attention.

"AHEM, MISS!" I coughed, trying again.

Nothing.

What? Was I just invisible now? Yoooohooooo! I'm talking. Why was nobody listening?!

Maybe I had to be louder.

"AHEM, MISS MINCHELL, PLEASE!"

Suddenly, a deafening silence filled the entire room and somehow it was like we were underwater. Perfect. It was SHOWTIME. At times like this, I really had to remind myself to take things slowly and breathe, especially since Bashir's jaw had dropped. He had no idea what was coming.

"Yusuf Ali Khan, this better not be a distraction."

Why did she always think the worst of me? What had I ever done in my life to even give her that impression?

"No, Miss," I shook my head. "Absolutely, definitely, 100%, in shaa Allah, not. This is serious."

She raised an eyebrow. So did everyone else actually. Why did they look so threatening?

"I actually have a present for you." I smiled my best smile. She took a step back and almost fell over. Like I said before, I have that effect on people.

"You do?" Miss squeaked, but then eyed me suspiciously. "It's not a sample of bird poop that you collected into a mayonnaise bottle again, is it?"

Oh man. She had her expectations sky high. "No, but I can definitely arrange that again if you like." Maybe it would sweeten her up again.

"Please don't."

Phew! That was hard enough to collect the first time.

"Well then, get a move on." Sairah piped up, pointing at the clock. "It's nearly break."

She had a point.

I slipped my hand into my trouser pocket and searched for my secret weapon. "It's definitely here somewhere." I dug deeper into my pockets. "It's definitely not that sticky, or that slimy or – aha! Ta-dah!"

The little chicken samosa was a teeny tiny bit crushed, but it still smelled of deliciousness if

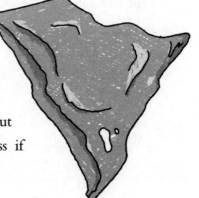

you sniffed it carefully. I had to sniff it twice to make sure it was still there. Yep, still there. I picked off the piece of fluff that was stuck on the pastry and passed it to Mustafa to pass it to the front to pass it to Miss.

"Why thank you, Yusuf." Miss practically jumped up with joy and pocketed the goodie in a little napkin like a present. "That's very kind of you,"

Bashir and Liam looked like they were going to be sick. The plan was definitely working. I'd have to thank Nanu for the tip later.

"You should eat it while it's still warm, Miss. That's how to get the maximum flavour."

Munching on Amma's special samosa in front of the class would be the best way to get back at Bashir for spoiling my morning.

"How's it still warm when school started hours ago?" Liam asked. He obviously wanted intel for next time. If he hadn't asked in front of the whole class, I could've kept that information classified. I guess sometimes you must spill some secrets for the greater good.

"I sat on it to keep it extra toasty."

The Dastardly Duo looked at each other and shook with fear.

I couldn't have asked for a better reaction.

"Oh, well I'm certainly looking forward to eating this

at dinner time on my own later."

True.

Miss Minchell had the right idea.

Revenge was a dish best served cold.

Yusuf: 1 – Bashir: 0

CHAPTER NINETEEN

"RE-VENGERS ASSEMBLE!" Aadam shouted at break-time from the corner of the playground, where our spot was. He was waving a gazillion pieces of paper in the air and jumping up and down.

Mustafa and I raced towards him. Mustafa even did a roly-poly, but because he rolled straight over a puddle, it wasn't as cool as it looked.

"Yuck," he said, as he shook off the water. "Yusuf swap jumpers with me. Mum is going to kill me. She told me twelve times yesterday not to do roly-polies after it rained."

Before I could even answer, Aadam interrupted.

THANK YOU, GOD!

"We have absolutely no time to waste. Break-time's nearly over and we have too much to do." He passed us a sheet of paper each. "Now feast your eyes on this amazing-ness. Have you ever seen anything this good?'

I took the paper and turned it over. "Just to be clear, we're not counting Jaffa cakes or chicken samosas, are -" but I stopped mid-sentence and gasped. "WOOOOOOOAAAAAAAAHHHHHH! THIS IS SOOOOO COOOOOOL! Like MEGATRON-SUPERSONIC-COOL!"

Before my very eyes was the world's best campaign poster ever. Somehow Aadam managed to stick my own face on Spiderman's body, and guess what? I wasn't just wearing any spidey-suit, it was the special edition IRON-SPIDER SUIT! He really had thought of everything!

"You look the COOLEST!," Mustafa jumped up and down and read. "Spider-bhai: With great power comes great responsibility, and I promise to be responsible! Vote for me or die at the hands of the enemy. The choice is yours."

"There's no way I'll lose with this!"

Aadaam gave us a fistful of posters each and ran towards the corridors inside.

"Come on, come on, come on!" he yelled. "We don't have much time!"

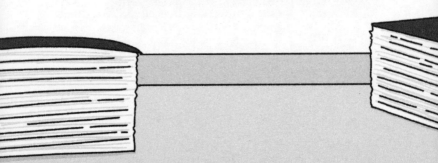

CHAPTER TWENTY

"We're too late," Aadam stopped in his tracks and all his posters scattered to the floor. "It's over."

"What do you mean…" But I couldn't even finish what I was saying, because plastered all over the Year 5 corridor was Bashir's HUGE face. He was everywhere, and I mean EVERYWHERE. No square-millimetre had been spared. Like a true villain, he had taken over and we couldn't even stop him.

Don't cry, Yusuf Ali Khan. Are you listening to me, eyeballs? DO NOT CRY. I command you!

"Do you want to be a leader who will lead the way?" Mustafa said.

"YES!" I cried. "That's all I want to be! I've worked my whole entire life for this. MY WHOLE LIFE!" My eyeballs weren't listening and they started leaking anyway. Make it stop. MAKE IT STOP!

"Oh, sorry, Yusuf." Mustafa said. "I wasn't asking you. I'm just reading Bashir's poster."

Oh.

"I knew that." I started reading the posters too. It was the only way I could hide my face without being detected. I rubbed my glasses with my sleeve so I could see a bit more clearly.

To make things worse, Aadam started reading out loud too. "Do you want a Captain that will not take no for an answer?"

"Erm, guys," Sairah's voice echoed through the corridor, making us jump. But strangely, she was

nowhere to be seen. She was obviously in spy-mode and obviously really good at it. "Maybe you should read it in your head? I mean, Yusuf's crying."

"I AM NOT!"

Why was she always so nosey? Didn't she have anything better to do?

I ripped a poster from the wall and read. It said: Do you want a future for 5B to be the greatest class

once again? Then vote for Bashir Ahmed on election day, and we promise that your life will never be the same again!

"Look at what he's promised," Aadam said seriously. "Free brownies, no more homework, non-uniform day everyday, and film Friday at the end of every week. What are we going to do?" Aadam shook his head. "I'm sorry, Yusuf. I tried my best with the posters. I thought they'd be enough."

"Is it over?" I really didn't want to say it. I almost couldn't even say it because the words were stuck in my throat and my cheeks were on red alert.

"No!" Mustafa said. "No way is it over. It's not over until we say it's over. And that's not right now, I'm telling you." He whipped out a Sharpie from his pocket. (Who carries a Sharpie in their pocket?) "We have a duty to tell the truth, the whole truth and nothing but the truth." He started scribbling on the poster. "Aadam, keep an eye out for teachers. Sairah, wherever you are, go away, and Yusuf, here." He passed me a black felt-tip pen. I really wanted the Sharpie, though. "Help me do this."

"Do what?"

"We owe it to our people to tell the truth."

And if you really want to know, this is what the truth looked like:

~~Free Brownies~~ Free Bruises

~~Film Friday~~ Thumping Friday

~~Non-Uniform Day~~ Black Eye Day

I guess it is true what they say when they say it: the truth hurts.

Literally.

CHAPTER TWENTY-ONE

Me and Mustafa had to run back to the classroom because the bell had gone, and we had only just managed to finish OPERATION: TELL THE TRUTH. We had to take the long way back to cover our tracks too, and we had only just managed to slip out of the corridor before everybody else had started spilling into it.

But something wasn't right.

Miss Minchell was nowhere to be seen.

"Do you think she's been kidnapped?" Mustafa asked Saleem. "Or abducted by aliens?"

"Where were you?" Saleem asked. He kept looking over his shoulder like speaking to us was an enormous crime. "Don't you know what happened?"

But before he could spill the beans, Miss stormed towards us. Her eyebrows were twitching and her lips were scrooged up. Behind her was Liam, hiccupping and rubbing his eyes.

If I wasn't making a mistake right now, I'd say that his eyes had been leaking too.

I grabbed Mustafa's arm and squeezed. He stared back in horror.

UH OH.

"GET IN THERE NOW!" Miss Minchell bellowed, throwing the door open. "Not one word, 5B, lest you feel my wrath!"

CHAPTER TWENTY-TWO

"I am not going to ask you again," Miss was pacing the classroom, looking carefully at each and every one of us. We were her prisoners, and we were in the firing line. Shots would be fired. I was sure of it.

But nobody spoke.

The clock was ticking, the wind was blowing and only her footsteps broke the silence. But still no-one came forward. If I was being honest, I think that actually made it worse.

"Somebody better say something," she continued. "Or else."

Correction: that definitely made it worse, and I definitely needed to pee!

"HOW DARE YOU?" she screamed again. Miss was looking at me, directly at me. Her hair was flailing all over the place like octopus legs, the walls were shaking, and she was definitely looking at me. She knows. SHE KNOWS! "HOW DARE YOU TAKE

SOMEBODY ELSE'S HARD WORK AND EFFORT AND VANDALISE IT?"

My bones turned to jelly. I tried to keep my head down to avoid eye-contact with Mustafa, but both of our legs were shaking so much that I had to risk it and see if he was okay, even if I died doing it. I slowly raised my head to peek. His eyes were red and his fists were clenched. He actually looked like he was going to be sick. AND IT WAS ALL MY FAULT. If Miss Minchell didn't murder him, his mum would. He didn't stand a chance!

"EYES THIS WAY. NOW!"

She was going to explode. SHE WAS GOING TO EXPLODE! LEVEL FIVE PANIC ALERT! MAN DOWN! MAN DOWN! SHE WAS GOING TO EXPLODE!

"How absolutely shameful. How disrespectful," she spat. "I expected better from a class like this. If the person who graffitied all over Bashir and Liam's posters doesn't come forward in the next minute, the entire class will lose their dinner-time for a week!"

There was a huge gasp.

Oh no she didn't!

Oh YES she DID!

Miss just threatened to hold the entire class hostage and all eyes were on me. If somebody didn't speak up soon, well, then the whole classroom would collapse under the crushing weight of mine and Mustafa's guilt.

I had to confess. I had to. It was bad enough for Miss to hate us, but the rest of the class too? No, I would never be able to live that down. I'd go down in history as a loser and life as I know it would be over.

I just needed to take a deep breath and say 'It was me. I did it. Nobody else. Just me.' At least that way Mustafa wouldn't be mass-murdered too.

"It was me. I did it. Nobody else. Just me."

WHO SAID THAT? No, seriously, WHO SAID THAT?

I stared in horror at Mustafa. His lips were moving, sound was coming out and he was speaking. I watched him in slow-motion. There he was, all alone, on his own, wearing his damp school jumper like a hero's cape and making sure that his voice had been heard clearly. Mustafa was confessing to MY CRIMES! SAY NO MORE, MUSTAFA, SAY NO MORE! I'm coming to save you!

But just as I was about to plead guilty in front of the jury, Mustafa sealed the deal. He slammed the final nail on his own coffin. He did the unthinkable.

"I know you think it's Yusuf too, but it wasn't. If he

did something like that, then you'd disqualify him from being Captain. So it was just me. Just me."

My heart sank to my feet and stayed there. My best friend was facing a life sentence and he had made sure that there was nothing I could do about it.

"GET OUT OF MY CLASSROOM," Miss Minchell yelled. "I'LL DEAL WITH YOU LATER, MUSTAFA!"

GULP. GULP. GULP.

CHAPTER TWENTY-THREE

Mustafa didn't come into school the next day or to the mosque, or the day after that, or even the day after that. He was gone and it was all my fault. Since Amma and Khala had taken mine and Aadam's tablets after the food fight, there was no way of even communicating with him to see if he was still alive. Something told me he wasn't. He was either dead or he'd been packed onto the first plane to Gambia. I thought they'd at least let me say goodbye. We were best friends after all.

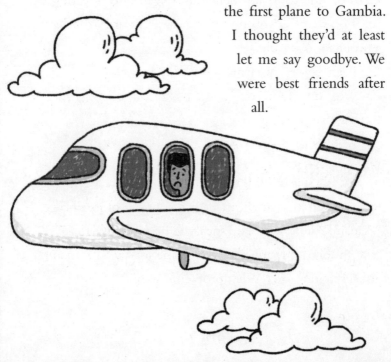

At school, I had bigger problems. Bashir and Liam, the Dastardly Duo, were up to something. I just didn't know what yet. I couldn't shake off the burn of their beady eyes when I hung up my coat and bag this morning. They were definitely watching me, but for what?

"Psssst, Yusuf," Saleem whispered at dinner time while we were making our way to the playground. "You need to hear this."

I followed his lead and he led me to Sairah's spot on the wall. I should have known. Wherever Saleem was, Sairah wasn't too far away.

"You, my friend," she began while nibbling on her khazoor (khazoors are delicious, sweet dates – eating a juicy one can fill you up for almost an hour). "You have a problem to handle."

Saleem folded his arms and nodded.

"What do you mean?" I asked. She couldn't be trusted. I knew that for sure.

"Yeah, what do you mean?"

"ARGHHHHHHHHHHHHHH!" I shrieked, trying to make sure that my heart hadn't leapt out of its ribcage. "Aadam! You have to stop sneaking up on us like that!"

"Oh sorry." He must have seen me follow Saleem and got suspicious too. "What problem?"

"Look, I hate to be the one to say it," she said slowly.
LIES LIES LIES.

"Get to the point already."

She definitely wasn't happy that I interrupted her. "Look, it pains me to say it. I hate being right all the time, you know that, don't you? But Yusuf, things are worse than they seem."

Oh no!

She dragged us to the corner of the wall where there were a million charts and graphs stuck on sheets of scrap paper. "Not only is Bashir still on the road to victory," she explained, pointing to the first graph.. "But everyone actually wants to vote for him now after what you two did."

"What does that even mean?" I think I knew what it meant. I just needed her to be 209.33% crystal clear.

Sairah rolled her eyes. "Look, we can't expose Bashir because he's trying to be a good person now and that's your fault. He's actually being really nice to everyone. He even gave me a packet of rasmalais, and they weren't out of date. I checked twice. I'm sorry, but I can no longer help you."

"What!" Aadam gasped. "But we gave you Oreos. We sealed the deal. Give them back then!"

"I can't," she shook her head. "They're already in my stomach and have probably been digested by now. Look, nobody votes for a bully."

"So why are you voting for him?" What kind of world were we living in?

"I meant you," Sairah snapped. "Why do you even want to do this after the amount of trouble you got Mustafa in? You should have confessed. It wasn't right."

"You don't understand." I lowered my voice and looked over my shoulder to make absolutely sure that we weren't being spied on.

For somebody who seemed to know everything about everybody, Sairah really didn't know anything at all.

"It's because of Mustafa I have to do this. I have to finish what he started, otherwise he died for nothing. If anything, I need to make sure I win now more than ever."

"He's dead?" Saleem asked. His eyes had started watering already.

"Yeah, I think so. He hasn't been on Roblox lately." I couldn't be sure though since I hadn't either, but he didn't need to know that. "You should vote for me in honour of his memory. He would have wanted that." I squeezed his shoulder because that's what Affa did when I got sad and somehow it made me feel a little better every single time.

93

"Forget that," Aadam hissed. "Why are you voting for someone who sellotaped you to a door last year, Saleem? And Sairah," he turned to her, pointing fiercely to the pen attached to her ear. "He told you that he used The 5B Times as toilet roll. You really want him to lead 5B?"

"Things have changed," Sairah said, sliding her pen from her ear and swinging it like a knife. Even I had to take a step back. "Bashir has changed."

"No, he hasn't." Aadam took her pen and waved it back at her. "You're starting to believe the lies that you've written. That's the problem with your newspaper. If you read something over and over again, you forget which part is real and which part is lies."

I nodded. "They're like Batman and Robin now, because you wrote them out to be heroes and now everybody believes it. Even you. But this isn't a movie. If Bashir becomes Form Captain, we're all goners. The power will get to his head and he'll destroy us all. You've created a monster."

Saleem looked confused and his head swung from us to his sister and then back again.

Sairah snatched her pen back and stood up. "Yeah, well, like it or not, Bashir is set to win and that's your fault and yours alone."

CHAPTER TWENTY-FOUR

"You've got three minutes to get changed, boys," Miss Minchell told us, as Mr Boakye pointed towards our changing rooms.

"Make it fast, lads," Sir said, rubbing his glasses and taking a seat.

Fast? Didn't he know he was in the presence of Yusuf Lightning Kh–

WAIT ONE SMELLY MINUTE.

Where on the whole of planet Earth, the Sun, the stars and the galaxies beyond was my P.E. kit?

NO NO NO NO NO NO NO! Tell me this was not happening! SAY IT'S NOT SO!

Where's my inhaler? WHERE ON PLANET EARTH WAS MY INHALER? Breathe, Yusuf. Breathe. Now calm the Jaffa cakes down. There had to be a reasonable explanation for this. There just had to be.

Maybe it was behind my coat?

I wiggled my coat, but nothing.

Maybe it was under the chair?

I peeked between the legs, but nothing.

Maybe it was in the bin?

No, only snotty tissues in there.

Maybe it just disappeared into thin air?

"Boys," Mr Boakye snapped. He closed the book he had been peering into. "Stop giggling and get yourselves over there already."

What? Giggling? Me? There was absolutely NOTHING funny about this situation. Unless…

HOLY SNOTBALLS! I should've known. There, in the corner of the classroom, was not my P.E. kit, but the culprits responsible for it going M.I.A. (this means Missing In Action, by the way – it's a spy word). Bashir and Liam, the Dastardly Duo, had the BIGGEST smiles on their faces. It was obvious. They'd been planning the attack since the morning. Only a fool would've missed it. I knew I felt their beady eyes on me. I should have been more alert.

I had to be cool. I had already messed up my chances with everyone's votes when Mustafa took the fall for me, so I needed to remind everyone what a cool, responsible, and respectable leader looked like in the face of huge life problems like this one.

"WAHHHHHHHHHHHH!"

WHO SAID THAT? WHO SAID THAT? Who on the whole of planet Earth, the Sun, the stars and the galaxies beyond, said that? And, more importantly, why was everybody staring at me?

I put my hand over my mouth.

Why was it open? WHY WAS IT OPEN? SAY IT'S NOT SO!

But my jaw had a life of its own!

"WAHHHHHHHHHHHH!"

I clamped down on my mouth harder, but I couldn't control it!

"Mr Boakye! Bashir and Liam have stolen my P.E. kit!" I grabbed my other hand and stuffed it in my mouth, but my tongue kept punching it back out!

"It's not fair. They've taken it and they won't give it back!"

NOOOOOOOOOOOOOO! Somebody stop me PLEASE! SOMEBODY SAVE ME FROM MYSELF, YAA RABB! SAVE MEEEEEEE!

"WAHHHHHHHHHHHHH!"

"YUSUF!" Mr Boakye shouted. A silence echoed through the changing room. "What's the matter with you?" Sir's eyebrows knitted together angrily. He did the pull-down-your-glasses thing to make his point.

My ears burned and my mouth finally closed itself, but it was too little, too late. Like it or not, it was coming. The world's worst-ever-news was coming, like a meteor that was aimed directly at me.

"You know the rules," he said, smiling like a silent assassin. "No kit? You know what to do."

CHAPTER TWENTY-FIVE

"Please don't make me do it, Mr Boakye," I clung onto the door handle for dear life, praying desperately that the sweat on my hands wouldn't make me slip away. "Please, please, please. PLEASE, PLEASE, PLEASE!"

Everybody was staring at us like they were seagulls and I was masala fish and chips! All my cool points had gone. Every single one of them.

"Yusuf, stop overreacting," Miss Minchell was back, and the two of them had tag-teamed up against me.

"Noooooooo, Miss, nooooooooo! They smell like feet – giant, pus-filled, warty feet!"

It was true! When Aadam forgot his kit, he had to wear a pair of mouldy Year 4 shorts and a yellow frilly vest for a whole hour. No way would they do that to me. Not if I could help it. They'd never get away with it - not with my eczema, I'm telling you.

In the distance, somebody sounded like they were vomiting. I would too, but I had BIGGER PROBLEMS TO FRY!

"Yusuf, you–," Mr Boakye said.

"Nooooooooo! you don't understand, sir." What was wrong with him? I hugged the door tighter and activated

HULK-MODE. I wasn't leaving. Nope, no way. Not me. "I can't touch any of that stuff. It's diseased. I'll catch something. I'll die. Do you really want that on your conscience?"

WHO WAS I KIDDING?! OF COURSE, HE'D BE HAPPY TO HAVE THAT ON HIS CONSCIENCE. WHO WOULDN'T?! ARGGHHHHHHH!

"Stop over-exaggerating," Miss Minchell rolled her eyes. Easy for her to say. "If you don't get a kit on soon, then–"

"I don't want to go," I yelled over her, trying to dig my heels into the door. "Don't make me. You can't make me, I won't go!"

"Well, we'll just call your mum, then," Miss Minchell finished, pushing the door open.

I swung forward. WAIT! Why was I moving? Oh man, I should have dug my heels onto the floor, not the door!

Before I could defend myself, Mr Boakye stepped in.

"Ring his grandmother." He smiled menacingly. "In fact, I'm just going to go call her now."

I paused, still clutching tightly to the handle.

"Is that a threat, Mr Boakye?"

Was it? Was it? I had to know!

"Yusuf, Yusuf, Yusuf," he said, shaking his head. "It's not a threat."

Phew.

"It's a promise," he finished.

ARRRRRRRRGGGGGGGGHHHHHHHH!

I let go of the handle and peeled myself off the door.

"Why would you ring home?" I asked. "Can't you see that I'm already on my way to the room of doom to die a painful death at your hands?" I groaned. "Lost Property, here I come."

The worst part was that I had to do the walk of shame in front of EVERYONE!

"He's a goner," Sairah hissed. "Inna lillahi wa inna ilayhi rajioon."

I mean, she wasn't wrong. There was no way I'd survive this.

CHAPTER TWENTY-SIX

"DON'T DO IT, YUSUF," Mustafa's voice was screaming inside my head, as I made my way to Lost Property. Even when Mustafa wasn't here, he was somehow still with me. "IT'S NOT WORTH IT. YOU CAN'T DIE LIKE THIS. THERE ARE BETTER WAYS TO GO!"

Every bone inside my body trembled; even my toenails were shaking. What choice did I have? All my superpowers were useless here and I was completely alone.

"If I don't do this," I whispered to the voice. "I'll suffer a fate worse than death. Nanu will send me back to Bangladesh and…. and…" I shuddered at the thought. "They'll make me eat Khatol and goat-heads."

I took a deep breath. You can do it, Yusuf. You can. Believe in yourself.

Mustafa's words were ringing in my head. "Remember when Saleem had to borrow some shorts? He got chicken pox the next day."

But the second I clicked the door open, Mustafa's voice suddenly disappeared, leaving me all alone.

'Don't say I didn't warn you,' I thought. Wait, why was I thinking like I was Mustafa and not Yusuf?

Focus, Yusuf! FOCUS!

I pushed the door open wider with my fingers.

CCCCRRRRREEEEEEAAAAAAKKKKKKK!

"H-h-hello?" My voice echoed into the room, the lights flickering slowly. "Is there anybody out there?"

Nobody answered.

Slowly, I tiptoed into the room, clinging onto the sleeves of my jumper for warmth.

It was cold.

Too cold.

I could hear a pipe dripping and there were cobwebs all over the walls. And, staring right at me from the middle of the room, were the lost P.E. kits of centuries past, festering gruesomely on the floor...

CHAPTER TWENTY-SEVEN

"Who stole my hutki?"

I was at home in Nanu's room. It was just the two of us and Nanu had trapped me in by barricading the door with her walking stick. Nobody was getting in or out.

"I didn't do it, Nanu. I promise." I couldn't move. Not because she had tied me up or anything, but because her room was so small and there was only a 10cm² floor space where she could hold me hostage.

"I believe you.... NOT!" She spat, spluttering fan juice all over me. GROSS! She got her gwa-fan bata (a little tiffin where she kept her precious edible goods) out from the folds of her sari and held it out like a grenade. Nobody, and I mean nobody, comes between Nanu and her hutki.

She sniffed behind my ear and under my armpit. "I can smell it all over you." She even sniffed my glasses after tapping them with her bony finger. "You don't fool me. If you're not careful, Eesoof Ali Khan, I will gobble you right up. Now where is it? What did you do?"

HOLY JAFFA CAKES!

"No, Nanu. You don't understand!" I tried to pull away from her, but her grip was too hard. For a tiny lady, she sure was strong. "It's the old P.E. kit. It was all stinky and they made me wear it and I nearly suffocated from the smell."

Nanu circled me. Well, actually, we circled each other. Like I said, carpet space.

"You expect me to believe that you came home from school with that delicious aroma of spices clinging onto you?"

"I smell like dead fish and radioactive Year 1 knickers, Nanu! I mean, who loses their, y'know, underpants at school?!"

107

"Exactly… oh wait." Nanu scratched her nose and scuttled towards her bed. "Here it is!" She pulled out a plastic bag of dried fishy parts from under her pillow and hugged it. "How did that get there?"

GROSS!

"Nanu, have you been sleeping with the fishes?"

Wait, why was I talking? This was the perfect moment to activate stealth mode and sneak out.

"EEEEESSSSOOOOOOOFFFFFFF!"

I froze. Oh man, I had almost made it!

"You're not leaving until I've counted every last one of them. How do I know you haven't taken any in secret?"

"Nanu, there's a million and more in that bag! I'm going to be late for mosque! I can't go smelling like this! Don't you trust me?"

"Of course… not." Nanu slowly spilled out the hukti pieces onto her bed. A huge cloud of skunk poison detonated above it and slowly, slowly, she counted them one at a time. "Anyway, while you wait, you can cover the smell with some of those sprays." She pointed to the corner of the room, where there was a little collection of bottles and nozzles. "Your ammu will be back soon so get to it!"

CHAPTER TWENTY-EIGHT

"IT BURNNNNNNNNNNSSSSSSS, NANU,"
I screamed. Why wasn't she listening to my pain?
"IT BURNNNNNNNSSS US!" My skin didn't
stand a chance. I tried to rub off the spray frantically.

"What's wrong, my little hutki?" Nanu ran over to me.

When I say 'ran', I mean that she took one wobbly step and came to my rescue, blowing on my arms.

"This is poison!" I squealed, holding up the bottle called Fabreze. "Are you trying to kill me?"

"This just smells like flowers, beta. You know, if you were made in Bangladesh like your sister, this would be no problem." Nanu took the spray bottle and inspected it. "What about this one?" She pulled out a purple one and spritzed it on me before I could even answer.

The stench clawed itself to the back of my throat and squeezed down on me. "It smells like the dentist," I coughed.

"What about—"

"Yusuf?" Amma poked her head into the room. Her eyes were all red and puffy. The stink had obviously got to her too! "What are you two doing?" She scanned the room and saw Nanu standing innocently behind me. "Look at the time, baba," she sniffed. "We have to go."

Without another word, Amma disappeared.

I quickly tried to inspect another bottle. Time was running out and there was no way I could go anywhere smelling like this.

"Come here, Eesoof," Nanu held out her hand, helping me off the floor and onto the bed. She sat down too and started rubbing my back just like she used to when I was small. It made me feel warm and fuzzy, and it always used to put me to sleep. "You've been really busy lately, haven't you?"

I hadn't told Amma that I was on a very important mission to regain our family honour. I wanted it to be a surprise, so it would make her extra happy. I was praying that there'd be some chicken samosas involved too.

Nanu kept on stroking my back. "You know, Eesoof, real leaders look after their own. If the whole world can speak well of you, what's the meaning if your own family can't?" Nanu's bottom lip wiggled.

"What do you mean?" Something wasn't right here.

"Since your sister left, the house has felt a little lonely. Even more so for your ammu. You saw how she was crying just now."

CRYING?! HOW DID I NOT NOTICE THAT?

"It would be nice to see you once in a while, beta," Nanu finished.

"You don't understand.. I have some V.I.Bs (very important business) going on. With mosque and school and homework and my Jaffa cakes, I don't really have much extra time."

"So, you're too busy to spend time with your ammu and nanu?" She put her hands on her hips and tilted her head sideways.

I straightened up. Affa had always told me to straighten up and look someone in the eye when you're about to tell them something really important. (Okay, so I did the straightening up bit, but I couldn't bring myself to look Nanu in the eye… yet.) "Look, I'm on the way to great things. GREAT HUGE POWERFUL things. I can't let anything get in the way."

But Nanu stopped stroking my back and pinched my cheek instead. "Keep an eye on your ammu, beta," she said quietly. "With your affa away and me getting old, who will she have left?"

Nanu got up and walked out of the room, leaving me entirely alone.

PLOP. PLOP.

Two little mothballs had rolled onto the floor.

WAIT ONE SMELLY MINUTE! NANU WASN'T STROKING MY BACK. SHE WAS RUBBING ME WITH MOTHBALLS ALL THIS TIME!

ARRRRRGHHHHHHH!

CHAPTER TWENTY-NINE

"Iron-bhai, we have a problem."

I filled Aadam in on everything that had happened, while trying to avoid Ustadh Saleh's laser eyebeams. Let me tell you, that wasn't easy.

"I've lost everything," I whispered, pretending to turn the page. "I've lost all my cool points, my chance at being Form Captain and, worst of all, I think I made Amma sad." I leaned back on the wall and yawned. "I don't think I'm cut out for this, you know. Making everyone happy is way too hard."

Aadam fixed his thoki just as Ustadh Saleh hawk-eyed us. "What did the Prophet (peace be upon him) say about smiling?" he asked loudly. Even the boy beside us jumped in shock.

Oh, I knew this one! Good shout. "He said that 'smiling in your brother's face is an act of charity'."

BOOOOYAAAAH!

Ustadh Saleh scowled and turned his head to someone else. Honestly, he should take the Prophet's advice sometimes. Only God knew why he was such a grumpy-pants all the time.

"Is that why you look like a human tomato today?" Aadam asked, mumbling into our safe zone.

"Nooo," I said, shaking my head. "That's because Amma dumped me in the bath before coming here. I don't know what's worse, smelling like fresh Epaderm or old kit."

"Anyway," Aadam continued. "We need to focus on the important stuff. You need to put all your energy into being Captain and you need to humiliate Bashir after the torture he's put you through. We need to make him pay for what he did. Forget about your mum. We can sort that out later."

What was he saying? "Forget about Amma?" I said a little too loudly. How can you forget someone you live with? "I don't think I can do that."

Ustadh's head snapped towards us again. Danger! Danger! Avert, avert!

"What does the Qur'an say about parents?" I half-yelled.

"Why did you ask me a hard one?" Aadam hissed.

"Errrm look after them because they're old?"

"Close enough – be the best to them, and to your mum because she…"

Saleem had asked Ustadh a question. Good timing. He was distracted for now.

"Look," I lowered my voice and put the book right in front of my face, so it was covered. "I need to figure out if I want to get my own back on Bashir or make Amma proud. I have a BAD feeling that the first one is going to get me in BIG trouble."

"I don't understand. Why can't you do both? Get revenge by beating Bashir and winning Form Captain, and then Khala will have to be proud of you. You'll have your honour back and you'll be the greatest leader 5B ever had. That's easy enough, since nobody's been a 5B leader before. It's simple."

Aadam didn't get it. There was a difference. I just didn't know how to explain it. If Mustafa was here, he'd know exactly what to say. I didn't want to admit it, but I missed Mustafa. I missed him A LOT.

"You have five more minutes, everyone." Ustadh Saleh called. "Saleem's mum has given him khazoors too. Make sure you all take one and pass it on."

I wiggled my bottom on the floor and stretched my legs to get comfortable. "I don't know about that, Aadam."

115

He shook his head as Saleem came around, passing everyone a little brown nugget each. They were the fattest and juiciest ones (yes!). I managed to sneak one for Amma and Nanu too.

I turned back to Aadam. "Something tells me that I'll be hearing from Affa and her Daffy Duck voice soon, especially after today."

Just the thought of it made my stomach drop to the floor.

Aadam looked a little bit scared. He looked over his shoulder twice to make sure she hadn't snuck up on us. It was no secret that Affa had put him in a headlock and tried to put him in the bin last summer. I'd be scared too. "She's not going to be happy, is she?"

Nope. Not. At. All.

CHAPTER THIRTY

"MUSTAFAAAAAAAA!" I yelled from across the yard, jumping about and waving. "YOU'RE ALIVE! YOU'RE ALIVE! YOU'RE ALIVE!"

He was putting a book back into his bag and HE WAS DEFINITELY BREATHING. I knew his mum wouldn't send him back to Gambia. I just knew it.

"HUGS LAW! HUGS LAW!" I ran like lightning and almost crashed into him. "Where have you been?" I rummaged through my bag and passed him a whole pack of Jaffa cakes.

"This is for meeeeeee?" Mustafa was jumping too. "No way! Yusuf, you're the best!" He shook the pack.

"Wait, are there ten in there or did you eat nine and a half like last time?"

"Would I ever do that to you?" Yes. Yes, I would. "I promise that there's a whole entire pack in there minus only two, but, to make up for that, I got you this."

Wait, what did I get him?

Mustafa's eyeballs became huge. "Whatisit? Whatisit?"

Oh great.

"Mustafa, you're not giving me room to look." Only God knew what I was looking for. I rummaged through my bag, looking for something, anything! "Ah ha! Here it is." I pulled out my khazoor from yesterday and squished it back into shape a little. "It's still fat and juicy, see?"

"Erm, you can keep that." Mustafa said, ripping open his Jaffa cakes and stuffing one in his mouth. "I have millions of those. Anyway, what did I miss?"

I filled Mustafa in on everything, from the smelly room of doom to Aadam's plan for world domination. He stared at me in horror throughout the whole story.

"Where did you go though? I thought you went missing."

"Nope," he said, chomping on his seventh Jaffa cake. "After the whole poster thing, I was so scared of going home. You know what Mum's like. I had to distract her somehow, so I was sick all over my jumper. It was gross and yellow and lumpy, but it did the trick."

"Coooooooooool."

I hadn't forgotten about the trouble I'd gotten Mustafa into, and it made me feel even worse that he had to wear his own gloopy sick to get himself out of it. That was extra gross.

My tummy was feeling a bit wobbly, and I had only just put my breakfast in there. That wasn't a good sign. "I'm sorry for being a rubbish best friend." There, I said it. It was about time too. "I didn't mean for it to get out of hand. I was going to confess, I swear. You just got there before me."

"Say no more," Mustafa nodded. He put his last Jaffa cake into his bag. "You're my friend. It's what friends do, right? Anyway what's the plan, Agent Khan? We're still going to win, aren't we?"

"We are?" I scratched my head. "I don't think we stand a chance."

"We don't have a choice, Spider-bhai." Mustafa grabbed his bag and leaped into action. "You don't just hand something like this to the enemy." He pointed at Bashir the Basher, who had just snatched a bag of cheese and onion crisps off a Year 3 kid. "You fight for what's right. The world is counting on you, Yusuf Ali Khan, so we need a plan."

No pressure!

CHAPTER THIRTY-ONE

Because we couldn't risk Mustafa getting into trouble again, the plan had to change and OPERATION: SUPERHERO was now ALL SYSTEMS GO!

If we wanted to be leaders, we needed to show 5B that we had the good stuff and that we were born to be the best.

We had already:

- given Saleem a SAFE chair when Liam swapped it for the one with wobbly legs (we gave Liam the wobbly one so he could taste his own medicine)

- rubbed the whiteboard for Miss before she even had a chance to (we probably should have waited until the end of the lesson because her nose-fumes and shaky fists told me she wasn't happy)

- intercepted three glue sticks from Bashir who had plotted to stick Mustafa to the floor (it looked

like he still wanted revenge after all)

• tidied all the books on the bookshelf and put them in colour order (we probably shouldn't have done this until we had finished our work either, but like all good leaders, we learn from our mistakes!)

• given everyone whiteboards to write their work onto to save paper and the planet (except it looked like our class did no work when we wiped everything at the end of the lesson – my bad)

And now we were on our most dangerous mission yet: we had to clean up a battleground. Yes, you heard right. We'd just had our Science lesson on materials and there was paper shrapnel, paintbrush darts, plastic-bottle drones, and cups of fizzy water, everywhere. Absolutely nothing, and I mean nothing, could possibly go wrong. Am I right?

"GIVE IT TO ME, BASHIR!" I yelled the moment Miss slipped out of the classroom. He had taken the fizzy cups that were both liquid and gas, and was trying to pour it down the sink. "CAN'T YOU SEE I'M TRYING TO BE HELPFUL?"

"I told Miss I'd pour out the water and she said yes to me and Liam, not you and Mustafa," Bashir shouted back, clutching onto three cups for dear life. "Stop butting in!"

"Yeah!" Liam grunted, trying his best not to drop any water. "Go do the paintbrushes! This is our turf!"

"You want to talk about turf?" Mustafa said, rolling up his sleeves. He was getting angry now. His entire body was shaking and the whole class was staring at us. Worse still, Sairah already had her notepad out and was scribbling away. "Well, I'll show you 'turf'!"

Mustafa dove into the corner and pulled out Liam's tray. "This, my not-so-friend, is your turf." He wiggled a bright picture of some grass and the sun that Liam had drawn two weeks ago. It was actually quite good, I had to admit.

"What?" Me, Bashir and Liam said together.

I knew that Mustafa was brilliant, but sometimes he was too much of a genius even for me.

"A 'turf' in the dictionary is a patch of grass, so that's not your turf, Liam," Mustafa yelled. "Go back to your own turf and give us the cups."

"YEAH! That makes sense!"

See? I told you he was brilliant.

"Erm, boys?" Miss Minchell must have slipped back in without us noticing. That would explain why the rest of the class was quietly tidying up and minding their own business. DRAT! "What's going on?"

"Nothing! Bashir was just giving us two cups of fizzy pop from his table to pour out." I went over to his desk and took THREE (not two) out of his hands. If you looked closely, the vein under his left eyebrow looked like it was about to explode. "Thank you very much, Bashir."

"No, thank you very much, Yusuf," he said through gritted teeth. It looked like he didn't want to get into trouble either. "How helpful and good you are. Here, have another one." Bashir PUSHED another cup into my hands and it spilled all over my jumper.

I'M NOT GOING TO CRY. CRY, I WILL NOT! I WILL CRY NO MORE!

Be cool, Yusuf. Be cool.

I caught my breath. Miss hadn't even been looking at us! She didn't witness any of Bashir's crimes! She was wiping the board! Who does that?

"Why thank you, Bashir," I stammered loudly. OPERATION: BE LOUDLY POLITE WHEN MISS WAS AROUND still had to go on, because that's what the best spies do. They take their missions seriously. "How kind you are."

"Isn't it lovely that you two are getting on?" Miss Minchell said. "I never thought I'd see the day."

CHAPTER THIRTY-TWO

Where was Aadam? Was he off? Was he sick?

Wherever he was, I'll tell you where he wasn't. He wasn't in the corner of the yard like he usually was. Nope, there was no Aadam-shaped being over there. Not at all. In fact, none of the Year 6s had been released from class yet. What was going on? I scanned the yard to double check. It was only the minions and us. Well, minus Mustafa. His mum made him ask for the work he missed.

I activated my handheld binoculars to investigate. They were literally 'handheld' because I held my hands over my eyes and zoomed across the playground. Sairah and Saleem were huddled over some sheets of paper, obviously stirring trouble. The Year 3s were playing The Floor Is Lava in the far corner, and Bashir and Liam were playing Piggy in the Middle with the Year 4 ball. Something told me that the Year 4s were being forced to play against their own will - unless there was another reason they were all screaming. Honestly, all they had to do was team up and form a wall of terror between them. Didn't they know that even Bashir the Basher wasn't Hulk enough to take them all on?

GRUMBLEEEEEEE!

What was that? I spun around to find the source of the noise. WHAT was THAT?

GRRRRUUUUMMMMMMLLLLLLEEEEE!

Oh wait, it was just my tummy.

"But you've just eaten dinner!" I told it. "How can you be hungry already?"

I guess that was the price I had to pay for giving Mustafa my Jaffa cakes.

Because my stomach seemed to have a mind of its own, I had to feed it quickly. If I didn't, silent reading after break wouldn't be so silent after all. Trust me, nobody wanted that.

I rummaged my pockets for something to nibble on:

Fluff – nope

Affa's snotty tissue from the day she left – nope

A pen lid – there wasn't much more to chew

Yesterday's khazoor – YES!

SWOOOOOOOOOSHHHHH!

ARRRRGGGGHHHHHH! A asteroid (or football) shot straight at me, missing me by 0.62825mm. But worse than that: my khazoor went soaring into the air.

"I'll save you!" I shrieked, diving for the little fruit. Everybody knew that the five-second rule didn't work outside! I stretched out my hand and just caught it by the tips of my fingers. "Phew, that was close!"

I brushed in gently, but before I could take a bite, Liam yelled at the top of his lungs. "YUSUF, NOOOOOOOOOOOO!"

CHAPTER THIRTY-THREE

"WHY ARE WE YELLING?" I shouted back

at Liam.

Obviously, he had lost the plot. There was no other explanation for it. Unless… that was what he wanted me to think. Was it? WAS IT? Was this some sort of secret plot to ruin my chances of 5B domination?

"Are you eating what I think you're eating?" Liam asked, pulling the football closer to him.

I should've known. After what happened in the classroom, this was definitely part of a secret plan to eliminate me. He was obviously trying to distract me from a trick that Bashir had schemed up, now that I was on my own with no Mustafa and no Aadam beside me. It all made sense now.

"What do you mean?" I asked. I had to keep him talking. The more he said, the more classified information he could leak. A super-spy like me had to always be in spy mode.

"I think you know what I mean," he said, backing away from me now. His eyes were glued to the fat, juicy khazoor in my fingers. "You wouldn't dare."

"I wouldn't dare?" I knew Liam hated eating anything that wasn't chips, but I didn't think he was that bad – unless he'd poisoned it? But he hadn't been anywhere near my pockets. I would've known about it if he had, wouldn't I? I nibbled the corner of the khazoor, just to double-check. It didn't taste poisonous to me.

"NOOOOOOO WAYYYYYYYYYYY!"
Liam shrieked. # "YUSUF, WHYYYYYYY?"

"It tastes nice." I nibbled a little more, becoming suspicious of the whole thing. "Here, you try."

But Liam shook his head and threw the football onto the floor. He smiled evilly and ran towards the wall where Sairah and Saleem were playing. "You're going to be in so much trouble," he called over his shoulders. "You shouldn't have done that. Your Allah is going to be so mad at you! I'm going to tell Him!"

"My Allah? Tell Him what?" It was official: Liam had lost the plot. The PLOT was LOST. I swallowed the rest of the khazoor quickly, but even so, something deep in my stomach told me that trouble was brewing.

I just didn't expect it to come so quickly.

CHAPTER THIRTY-FOUR

"YUSUFFFFFFF! WHYYYYYYYY?"

Mustafa was running across the playground like he was getting chased by a Pac-Man that wanted to gobble everything in sight. His hands were waving so frantically, it was hard to know if he was human or half-octopus. "WHAT HAVE YOU DONE? SAY IT'S NOT SO!" he yelled. "SAY IT'S NOT SO!"

"I DIDN'T DO ANYTHING!" I shouted back. "IT WASN'T ME!"

Why was everyone treating me like Enemy Number #1?

But wait, what was that flapping in his hands?

NOOOOOOOOOOOOOO! PLEASE, GOD!

Tell me that it wasn't what I thought it was. No way was this good news!

Mustafa finally hurtled to a stop. "Yusuf, what did you do?" Before I could answer, Mustafa began reading, his fingers shaking as he did it.

WHAT A SILLY SAUSAGE

YUSUF ALI KHAN, the infamous poster-destroyer and somosa muncher, has proven himself to be 5B's true villain by devouring a wrinkly, burnt sausage after a double dare by Liam Bates at dinner time today.

WHAT?! NO WAY! I held tightly to Mustafa because my knees were suddenly jelly. How could I do something so – WAIT!

"I didn't do it! It wasn't me!" I snatched the paper from Mustafa, but I couldn't make it out. My eyes! Somebody's meddled with my eyes! How do I stop them from leaking? WHY, GOD? WHY? "WHO WOULD MAKE UP SOMETHING LIKE THIS?" I tried reading it again, but my brain had turned to smush.

"Give it here," Mustafa patted my back and took The 5B Times from my hands. "Let me read it. It's… it's… it's better for you to know, but prepare yourself for the worst. This isn't going to be easy."

But I like things to be easy!

My cheeks began to burn because slowly, a million eyeballs across the playground turned in my direction.

"Hit me," I whispered. It was better to get it over and done with, right? RIGHT?!

Mustafa took a deep breath. "You know I'm here for you, man. Where was I? Oh, yeah. 'It was reported by an eyewitness source that Khan nibbled, not once, not twice, but monster-munched his way through what sources call a cocktail sausage.'"

"A cocktail sausage!" I could see a Year 4 shaking her head at me. "I don't even like tails! That wasn't me, I swear!

Mustafa continued. "'He even said that it was 'yummier than chicken samosas.'"

"Who would say such evil things?" I cried, rubbing my glasses.

"An eyewitness close to the scene reported that it wasn't the first time Khan had gotten friendly with a pig. 'In Year 2, he really ate a Peppa Pig sweet! I saw it with my own eyes.'"

"I was just a kid!" I squealed.

"One time, in mosque, our sources state that he nibbled on a hot dog!" Mustafa gasped. "I remember this!"

"IT WAS HALAL! You gave it to me!" Why didn't he remember the most important part of that story?!

"This shocking scandal—"

"Stop, Mustafa. Stop. My heart can't take it anymore." Somehow, I was on my knees. I didn't even have the strength to stand up for myself.

"I'm doing this for your own good, Yusuf. 'This shocking scandal comes during the most important time of life at Western Primary. Here at The 5B Times, we're not one to tell porkies, but with the

Form Captain elections taking place on Friday, the question remains, can we really trust a man who lies about chicken samosas?'"

CHAPTER THIRTY-FIVE

"I didn't believe it for a second," Aadam whispered, giving me a wet paper towel.

We were in the toilets, hiding out. The yard was no longer safe for a fugitive like me.

"Wait, didn't you shout to the entire dinner hall that Yusuf wasn't your cousin and that you didn't know him?" Mustafa said. He still had the newspaper in his hands, and was using it as a fan.

"You what?"

Aadam shook his head and turned his back to the hand-dryer. "That was before I read it, silly. I knew Yusuf wouldn't lie about chicken samosas like that. Not if he knew what was good for him, anyway."

"What am I going to do?" I asked them. "I've been ruined. Nobody will ever trust me again, and everything we worked so hard for this morning has gone down the toilet."

FLUSHHHHHHHHHHH!

"Oh sorry - I was just, erm, taking care of business." Mustafa had used The 5B Times to protect himself from touching the handle. I guess it was useful for something. "There was a gross mark in there. I think Saleem tried to flush his chocolate pudding again. You know how much he hates the school ones."

"Super gross!" Aadam wiggled his whole body, like he was trying to shake the germs off.

"What do we do now?" I asked. "How could Sairah write this? She's supposed to be my friend! She needs to fix it before it's too late."

"Let's tie her up and burn her on the steak." Aadam suggested.

But Mustafa shook his head. "Even the steak doesn't deserve that. Mum always says never to trust the people behind the papers. We need to go to a higher power. We need to teach her a lesson. We have to tell a grown-up. Then we can shut her down, once and for all."

"How is that helping anybody?" Aadam squeaked. "Sairah's had that paper running since she got her pen license. You'll never be able to shut her down. If anything, she'll call you a snitch and make things two million times worse. You know what they say: don't try to boss a boss woman, otherwise you'll get thrown in the bin."

"Who said that?" I asked. I'd definitely heard that one before.

"Your sister – last year, remember? That was before she

and Rabia Affa dumped me in the recycling bin. I had to tip myself over and crawl out before the binman threw me in the lorry. It was a close call."

"Yeah, those were the good old days."

"Somebody's coming! Quick! Hide!" Mustafa squeaked.

We jumped into one cubicle, piggybacking on each other. Mustafa was at the bottom, because he was the strongest, and I was at the top, because I could cling to a door like Mowgli to a vine. Poor Aadam was sandwiched in the middle. If he moved too much, either Mustafa would fall and we'd be discovered, or it would rain eczema skin-flakes. I wasn't sure which one would be worse for him.

"Are you sure he had a sausage?" The door creaked open and Bashir's voice trailed in.

"100%. Me mam makes them all the time." Liam must have come in after him. "They're the cocktail ones, but his one was a bit burnt and crispy."

Somebody turned the tap on, while somebody else trickled. SUPER GROSS.

"Guys," Mustafa hissed. "I can't hold on much longer!"

"You have to!" I whispered back. "You can do it."

But he was wobbling! One wrong move and we'd go straight into the toilet bowl!

"Why would Yusuf do that? I don't get it. He's trying to win his honour back. I don't think he would do that."

There was a long pause.

"I saw it with my very own two eyes." Liam called over the sound of the taps. "At first, I thought it was cat poop. Me step-dad's cat Nala plops like that."

"Anyway, you know what that means though, don't you? Yusuf Smelly Khan has absolutely no chance now, and I'm going to make sure of it."

All of a sudden, Mustafa's wiggling stopped. We were like statues, waiting for them to leave. When the door creaked open again, and the toilets were empty, we wriggled down. Instead of being all sweaty, and huffing and puffing, Mustafa stood firm like only heroes did.

"Re-vengers," he said seriously. "It's time to rumble."

CHAPTER THIRTY-SIX

"You owe me big time!" I said, waving yesterday's 5B Times in Saleem's face (I was too scared to do it to Sairah - you would be too. Don't lie). I had written and rehearsed an entire speech 106 times last night, with the help of Sheikh Google and Nanu, and I was definitely going to tell her exactly what I thought! "How could you betray me like that? I'm your brother from another mother. Have you no shame? What will people say?"

"I know," Sairah said, looking down. "I made a mistake. I know you wouldn't do something like that."

I had it all planned out: me and Aadam would tag-team them both and, because we couldn't trust Sairah, we'd have to wait until she was caught off-guard and then Aadam would pretend to try and choke-slam her (obviously he wouldn't actually do it because Sairah would realistically kill us). While she was distracted, I'd grab her notebook, run away to the opposite end of the playground where she couldn't hurt us, and we'd hold it hostage. Then we'd declare war – wait! What did she just say?

"Huh?"

Something wasn't right here.

"She said she's sorry." Saleem nodded.

"No, I didn't," Sairah corrected him, her fingers reaching for her pen and notepad. "I just said I made a mistake. There's a difference."

Well, that went much better than I ever dreamed it would.

"Why would you write something you don't even believe in?" I asked, trying my best not to rip the paper to 83 gazillion pieces. "It doesn't make sense."

"You've done Yusuf dirty and you haven't even said sorry!" Aadam used my body as a shield as he spoke. Honestly, was there anybody out there who wasn't scared of her?

"It was just a really good headline." Sairah said, pulling the pen lid again like she'd LEARNT NOTHING. "I didn't want it to go to waste."

ALL THIS FOR A HEADLINE! WHA- WAIT - WHYYYYYYYYYYY?

"SAIRAH!" My breakfast nearly burst out of my stomach. I had to physically hold it back. "You don't know what you've done. You've ruined everything! You don't even care. You haven't even said sorry. You do this all the time! It's not fair!"

Aadam put his hands on my shoulders. "Calm down, Spider-bhai. It's not too late to fix it."

"Yes, it is!" I yelled. My head was hurting, my tummy was wobbly and my glasses were slipping off my face. "Yes, it is! All I wanted was Amma and Nanu to be proud of me after that stupid food fight. Amma misses Affa and this was the ONE THING that would remind her of our honour and you ruined it, Sairah. You ruined it all!"

"Look," Sairah began, but she didn't say anything.

They were all staring at me like a booth (AKA a ghost) had taken over me.

"No, you look." If she wasn't going to finish that sentence off, then I was ready. "You can't just make up stories like that. You'll never know what it's like to be the one being lied about. I had one shot and you wrecked it, and there's nothing we can do about it."

But Mustafa had almost-magically appeared out of nowhere.

"Well," he said. "We've actually got a plan."

CHAPTER THIRTY-SEVEN

"The Masked Trickster?" I said slowly, barely believing my ears. I watched Sairah in awe, as she pulled out a huge fact file from her bag. It was filled with pictures and newspaper clippings and multicoloured stickies galore. "YOU know HIM?"

"Not exactly," Sairah said, opening the pages and spreading them across the ground. "I've been tracking him for the past two years. He might be a complete mystery, but that doesn't mean he hasn't left clues behind. Nobody (apart from me) is that perfect."

I rolled my eyes. Only Sairah would think that. (And maybe Saleem too.)

"Woah," Mustafa breathed, picking up one of the pictures and examining it. "You must have hundreds and thousands of intel on him. Nobody's ever dug up this much dirt before."

"Let's cut to the chase, shall we?" Aadam whispered, looking around. He was right. We were beginning to attract attention from the others in the yard. If we were going to execute this, then we needed the element of surprise on our side. "So, what does all this mean?"

We all hushed, making sure that the coast was clear.

"It means..." Saleem started. "Wait, what does it mean?"

Sairah lifted the book and pointed to the picture of the empty toilet rolls. "If we manage to pull off the biggest prank the school has ever seen, then the four of us will be legends. Bashir will be humiliated; you'll get the votes and being Form Captain will be just the beginning. There's no telling what we'll be capable of."

"Wait, there's five of us," Aadam said, pointing to each one of us. "Why didn't you count Saleem?"

"I did." Sairah said. "Me, Mustafa, Saleem and Yusuf."

Before Aadam could interrupt again, Sairah shushed him.

"We don't have time," she continued, ignoring him.

"But how are we going to contact someone who hasn't ever been seen?" I asked. Something didn't add up here. "For all we know, he could have been in Year 6 last year and he's already gone."

"Who says it's a 'he'?" Sairah snapped.

Mustafa nodded. Whose side was HE on anyway?

"Like I said, legend has it that trickster vanished without a trace, but that's not actually true." Sairah flipped to a copy of an old 5B Times. It was written in crayon and had 'MYSTERY' all over it. "Look." She pointed at a picture of a card with Batman's Joker on it. "Rumours of the Masked Trickster go way back before our time. Even Mustafa's sister knows about the pranks."

"You have a sister?" Aadam asked. His jaw dropped. "I didn't know that!"

"Yeah, she's really old, that's why." Mustafa scratched his head. "I think she's nearly 19."

"That's not old!" I laughed. "Affa's 26 and that's prehistoric. She's a dinosaur and she was alive before Google."

"Annnnnnnyway," Sairah continued. "It looks like the prankster isn't one person. It's passed down, so when someone leaves, the next chosen one takes over, but their identity is hidden, and they have to be worthy." Sairah looked at each and every one of us seriously. "The Masked Trickster could be among us right now."

"Are you telling me that we're in the presence of greatness?" Aadam gasped.

Sairah shushed him again. "There's a common pattern. If you want to summon him, you have to leave a snack behind the Joker graphic novel in the library."

Aadam jumped up, like he'd suddenly had an electric shock. "We have a library?"

Mustafa shook his head. "It's next to the classroom with the tadpoles."

"WE HAVE TADPOLES?!" Aadam slapped his forehead. "What even is this place?"

"Anyway," Mustafa continued. "I know where the Joker book is. I just put it back last week. Leave that with me."

"Thanks, Mustafa." I patted him on the back.

"I'll go now. Maybe we can meet up after school."

"Be careful," Saleem whispered. "May He make it easy for you."

I said the three Quls and spat on Mustafa.

"What was that for?!" Mustafa wiped the shot of gloop between his eyebrows.

"He's protecting you obviously," Aadam nodded, shielding his own eyebrows from me.

"You're not meant to spit on him!" Sairah got dangerously close to me. "You're meant to do this!" She blew the biggest raspberry, raining slop all over my face.

"The bell's going to go any minute. I need to get a move on." With that, Mustafa turned back and ran towards the library.

It was too late to change our minds now and God only knew what wildness we'd unleashed.

I didn't want to admit it to anyone, but something in my stomach was turning… and it wasn't the long lost lechu I'd found in my pockets.

CHAPTER THIRTY-EIGHT

"YUSUUUUUUUUUUUUUUUFFFF! WAAAAA AIIIIIIIIIIIIITTTTTTTTTTT!"

It was home time, but for some reason Mustafa was running down the hall like a flesh-eating zombie was chasing him with an axe.

I ran back towards him.

"Did you make contact?" I shouted.

It had to be the Masked Trickster. Nobody else had that kind of power over Mustafa (except for his mum and his Lord obviously).

"You have to go to the library now! You don't have much time!" His voice echoed through the corridor. "He's waiting for you. I saw him! It's time!"

MEGA GULP.

"You saw him? It's a him! What did he look like? You're coming with me, right? Right?"

Please say yes. Please say yes. Please say yes.

"No."

OH MAN.

"I can't. Mum's waiting for me." He slammed to a stop and almost tumbled over. "I have to go, but Yusuf, listen." He looked around to make sure that there were no witnesses. "This is it. This is the moment you've been waiting for.

My stomach dropped. I didn't know if I had the guts to do this on my own.

"One more thing, Yusuf."

"Anything, anything for you, my brother, my bhai, my best friend." Wait, were my eyes leaking?

KHAAAAATHOOOOOOO!

Mustafa launched a humongous spitball that splattered across my glasses and nearly knocked me off my feet.

SUPER GROSS.

"For protection, man. May He keep you safe." Mustafa zipped his jacket and ran towards the door. "In shaa Allah, I'll see you soon."

I wiped the spit from my glasses and took a deep breath. It was time to find the face behind the Joker.

Ready or not, I had to go.

CHAPTER THIRTY-NINE

Everybody in school (apart from Aadam) knew that our library was one of the coolest habitats on planet Earth. I'm not joking either. Because of the rickety windows, the climate was always cold and it felt like an igloo, even in the middle of summer. Like I said, it was SOOOOOO COOOOOOL. I just wish we were allowed in there more. There was a huge rainbow of books to choose from, squishy beanbags that sucked you into another dimension, a whole table filled with clickity computers and even a little tray of colour-your-own bookmarks. What's not to love?

But today was different (in a bad way).

Today my heart had scuttled, all lizard-like, right the way up to my throat. If I wasn't careful, it would crawl straight out.

I opened the door slowly, trying hard not to make it creak. The blinds were down, and it was getting dark. This wasn't a good sign. Not at all.

Taking a deep breath, I stepped into the Danger Zone.

"You can do this, Yusuf. You can. I have faith in you." I had to say it out loud. I don't know why, but it made me feel better.

Suddenly, the windows rattled, and the wind slapped against the blinds. Obviously, there was a ghost here somewhere. There had to be. That was the only logical explanation.

"Yusssssssuuuuuuuuuuuuuuuuuuf…"

I spun around. WHO SAID THAT? WHO SAID THAT? WHO ON THE WHOLE OF PLANET EARTH, THE SUN, THE STARS AND THE GALAXIES BEYOND SAID THAT?

I backed into a corner for protection. Stop itching, Yusuf. Stop itching! You're going to fall apart! Little skin particles were already flaking to the floor!

"Yuuuuuussssssssssssuuuuuuuuuuuuuuuuuuf…"

It had to be in my head. I had just imagined it. Yeah, that was it. My mind was playing tricks on me. That was all.

Right? RIGHT?

I crept towards the bookshelves, where I knew the prankster would be waiting.

"Yussssssssuuuuuuuuuuuuuf…"

I WASN'T IMAGINING IT and I NEEDED TO PEE! RIGHT NOW!

153

Crossing my legs tightly, I recited Ayatul Kursi.

"Yussssssssuuuuuuuuuuuuuuf…"

It was the Masked Trickster. He was saying my name to scare me. I knew I couldn't trust him. Shifting the books on the shelf closest to me, I peeked through to try and spy on him. What I saw next would stay with me for the rest of my life, I was sure of it.

There, in the far corner of his lair, all alone and resting in the shadows, was the Masked Trickster. His face was covered by a hood that could have only been stolen from the Grim Reaper himself.

My whole life flashed before me: Dad leaving, Affa eating my Jaffa cakes, and Amma and Nanu crying into each other's saris. Like it or not, I had a family to save. It was now or never. This was the moment I'd been waiting for.

Like all heroes in their time of great need, I took another deep breath and stepped forward, revealing myself to the Trickster.

CHAPTER FORTY

"Oh great prankster," I began. I cleared my throat, making sure that my voice didn't shake. "Oh your prankness, I come to you as your minion because I need help desperately. Will you support me, oh masked one of the tricking kind?"

I stepped forward to catch a closer look, but the shadow man only shifted further into the darkness. The mysterious figure had his back to me. If I hadn't known I was in the presence of the grand high trickster, then I probably would've mistaken him for Batman.

"Erm…" I had to try harder. He wasn't budging, and I had to get a move on before Nanu went ape in the car park (she sometimes did that when she hadn't seen me for a long time - yes, she actually loves me THAT MUCH). Let's try again. I raised my voice. "Oh maker of legends, tickler of nose-hairs, thrower of toilet roll, SHOW YOURSELF!"

The being took a step forward (well, backwards for him).

"Thor nam kheetha," he whispered behind his hood.

HOLY SNOTBALLS! The thing could speak Bengali. IT SPOKE BENGALI. I'M GOING TO DIE! IT'S GOING TO KILL ME IN MY OWN LANGUAGE!

Trying my best not to throw the nearest chair at it, I steadied myself. I'd have to answer. After all, I needed the help, not him.

"My name is Yusuf Ali Khan, Year 5, Miss Minchell's class. I'm almost ten years old." Okay, so he didn't ask for all of that information, but when you've got the FEAR, it's hard to stop throwing up words. "When I grow up, I want to be an astronaut, a policeman or a human mango." There, I said it. My whole future. Now he had to keep me alive.

"What is it you seek from me, Spider Bhai?" His voice was low and scratchy. "What quest are you on, oh minion of mine?"

Hold on one smelly minute.

"AADAM! You're the masked prankster!" I reached over to him and pulled his hood down. "NO WAY! My whole life is a lie. I'VE BEEN LIED TO MY WHOLE ENTIRE LIFE! I DON'T EVEN KNOW WHAT'S TRUE ANYMORE! Spider Bhai, my backside." I shook my head and rubbed my glasses to make sure I wasn't dreaming. "I can't believe it!"

"Believe what?" Aadam blinked.

"That you're the famous Masked Trickster! You had us fooled all this time!"

Now it was Aadam's turn to shake his head. "What are you on about? I'm not him. Look." He stuffed his hands in his pocket. "It's in here somewhere, I swear." He pulled out a trail of Jaffa cake wrappers, a snotty tissue, five rubbers, a half-eaten pen, and then… "Aha! Here it is!"

The letter was all crumpled.

It read:

A true masked prankster never exposes his identity. Like magicians, we are a sacred kind and we never reveal our secrets. Know that the masked trickster lives among you and that Bashir is our enemy too. If it is vengence you seek, find it on Election Day. Just make sure that the Basher himself is the second speaker, not the first ... or else.

CHAPTER FORTY-ONE

"Woah. I can't believe it." I collapsed onto the nearest squishy beanbag, re-reading the note again and again. "All this time, I thought he was just a myth and legend, but here is living proof that the prankster lives."

"I know," Aadam said, zipping his hoodie up properly this time. "We all thought he had disappeared off the face of the earth, but he was just biding his time like Thanos. We should laugh evilly. I always wanted a reason to do that. MUHUHAHAHAHAHAHA!"

I sunk deeper into the beanbag. Was Aadam really the trickster? Was he just trying to hide his identity? I inspected the note again. "Who else hates Bashir?"

Aadam paused from his evil laugh. "Everyone. MUHAHAHAHAHAHA! If he's in Year 6, it'll probably be passed down to your class when we leave this summer. You can investigate then. MUHAHAHAHAHA!"

"Guys?" Mustafa suddenly popped out of a bookshelf!

"ARRRRRGHHHHHHH!" Aadam screamed, nearly choking on his evil laugh.

"How long have you been here for?" I squeaked, peeking out from behind the beanbag.

"A while," Mustafa smiled. "Anyway, do you think this is a good idea? I have a bad feeling about this."

Before I could say anything, Aadam answered for me.

"What do you mean? Do you have any idea what Bashir is capable of? He's a big bully! He'll ruin everything. All he ever does is try to humiliate everyone and make them feel like a loser. There's no way we can leave the fate of 5B in his hands – not on my watch."

"Yeah, but…" Mustafa came away from the bookshelf and flopped into the beanbag next to me. "Isn't that what you're planning to do?"

"Not in the slightest. It's not the same thing at all." I said. "We're only ruining everything for him so he doesn't ruin everything for us. It's for the greater good," I finished with a nod.

"Exactly!" Aadam agreed.

"I don't know, Yusuf." Mustafa took the note and shook his head. "I don't think this is the way to get back your honour."

I didn't want to admit it, but something deep deep deep inside me told me… he was right.

I took a breath and looked him in the eye. Sometimes, he reminded me a bit of Affa. "I don't have a choice."

Aadam jumped up. "We have to go, or Mum and Khala are going to send out a search party. Don't worry, Mustafa. We got this! Yusuf's going to go down in history as the greatest leader Western Primary has ever had, Bashir is going to go down full stop, and we're going to rule the world! It's settled." He pulled up his bag and his hood. "My mum always says that sometimes you have to be cruel to be kind. We must do what's best for 5B by any means necessary. Right, Yusuf?"

I looked at Mustafa, then to Aadam and then back at Mustafa. "Right."

As we ran towards the yard quickly, something in the pit of my stomach was churning.

CHAPTER FORTY-TWO

"HUGS LAW! HUGS LAW! HUGS LAW!" I squealed, before blasting into Affa like a hurtling asteroid. "When did you get here?"

We were in the kitchen, and Affa was sniffing a samosa to check if I had breathed on it.

"A few hours ago." Umar Bhai said. He was picking his beard for crumbs. He was **SOOOOO COOL.** If I had a beard, I'd stash my Jaffa cakes in there. "We thought we'd pop by for a long weekend. That's if you'll have us, Yusuf?"

I pulled up a chair next to Affa, stealing her scarf from behind it. "That depends…" Like lightning, I wrapped the scarf around her, being careful not to squeeze her to death. I'd need her alive for the next bit. "What's in it for me?"

"YUS–" Affa began, giving me the daggers, but Bhai interrupted her. Good thing too, because clearly I had drunk too much Capri Sun. Obviously, I had lost the plot if I was holding a certified assassin like Affa hostage. Didn't I know what she had done last summer?

"Listen, listen, leave it to me." Umar Bhai drew up a chair and closed his hands together. This was serious business. "I'm about to make him an offer he can't refuse."

I drew the scarf a little tighter around Affa, because she had started sipping her chaii. I had to be extra careful though; one wrong move and she'd throw the scalding deliciousness at me. If she did, I'd have no choice but to catch it in my mouth and swallow the creaminess, steaminess and dreaminess whole. You know me, I'm always about the greater good.

Bhai cleared his throat.

"Make it worth my while," I said. Bhai needed to go big or go home. He was on my turf now.

"Are you done?" Affa piped in, blowing her tea. "I told Nanu I'd make her some tandoori chops."

"Not yet," I patted Affa on the head to calm her down (but I think that had the opposite effect). "She's my only sister." I told Bhai. "I'm not going to give her up without a fight."

Bhai scratched his chin and sat up. "A little birdie told me that you're a Krispy Fried Chicken f-"

"SOLD!"

"What?" Affa yelped, almost falling off her chair (good thing I had tied her up). "He hasn't even finished his sentence! How do you even know what he's about to offer?"

"HUSHHHHHHHHHH" I hissed, putting a stern finger on her lips, and giving her a noo-noo so she didn't give me a black eye. "Let the boss speak." I turned to Bhai quickly. "Affa sometimes doesn't know what's good for her. Ignore her." I went to give her a little tap to remind her who was in charge now. After all, she wasn't the man of this house anymore. ARGH! By mistake, the tiny force of my fingers made Affa spill half of her chaii all over her jumper.

Oh no!

"Let me help!" Umar Bhai shot out of his chair as Affa squeaked, "I just bought this yesterday, Yusuf!"

"NO NO NO! YOU SIT DOWN." I scrambled to my feet. "SHE'S MY SISTER. SHE'LL BEAT ME UP not you. Don't be a hero."

Affa's face was turning into both a tomato and a tornado.

INITIATE DAMAGE CONTROL! INITIATE DAMAGE CONTROL NOW!

I dragged Affa's scarf to soak up the spilled tea, but she gave a little yelp because I HAD TIED HER TIGHTER TO HER OWN CHAIR!

"I think," Umar Bhai began.

"No! Thinking makes it worse!" I yelled. TOO MUCH PRESSURE!

But Affa had had enough. She stormed out of the chair, tearing away her scarf like only the HULK could. She snatched my entire body and dragged me down onto my chair.

OUCH! MEGATRON OUCH!

"Erm, Affa?" I tried to pull myself from her grip, but I was trapped. "This…" I struggled. "Kind of," I gasped. "HURTS!"

I searched for help. WHERE'S MY NANU?

PROTECT ME PLEASE! NANUUUUUUUUU!

"Nope, not getting involved, not me," Bhai said quickly, escaping through the door.

"DON'T LEAVE ME ALONE WITH ~~IT~~ HER!" I screamed, trying to wiggle away.

But it was too late. Affa had evolved into a raging bull and Bhai had left me alone.

CODE RED! CODE RED!

CHAPTER FORTY-THREE

"Yusuf Ali Khan." Affa had used her scarf to tie me to the chair and stuffed the ends of it into my mouth. It was so tight that I could barely move (or breathe).

"I've got a bone to pick with you."

I spat the tassels of the fabric out. "Afffffaaaaaa noooooooooo! Don't take my bones!" I squealed, as she grabbed the cling film. "I need those to grow! Why? WHY?

WHYYYYYYYYY?"

Affa had tied my hands behind the chair, so it was even harder to wriggle. There was a big squelch as she rolled out the cling film. That was NOT good. Escape mode had to be activated.

I quickly searched the table for something sharp enough to cut me loose:

Teaspoon - too blunt

Sugar - not spicy enough

Hijab pins - too far away

Dath keelai (I think this is called a toothpick) - perfect!

I tried to launch myself across the table, but the snake coils of Affa's trap kept me rooted to the spot.

"What are you doing?" Affa asked, peering at me through the cling film.

"What am I doing? WHAT ARE YOU DOING?" Had she lost it completely? "Why do you have cling film? Will you suffocate me? Manchester really has brought out the meanie in you!"

"I was going to use it to refrigerate the tandoori chops, but maybe I should tape your mouth with it," Affa snapped, raising her eyebrows. She stared at me for 37.9 seconds looking woozy, like she'd discovered an extra ear on my face. "I think I'm going to be sick."

How rude!

"Well, if I'm ugly, then so are you because everybody says I look like you so there!" I flopped back against the chair and sighed.

Affa blinked at me. Not just any blink. It was the DEATH BLINK – one that silently said 'BOY, IF YOU DON'T SPILL THE BEANS, I WILL BEAT YOU BLACK AND BLUE' and that wasn't a risk I was willing to take.

"Okay, okay, you got me." I guess it was time to face the truth. "I know Amma told you to come and 'fix' me."

"You do?"

"Yeah, I heard her talking to Nanu the other day."

"You did?"

"Yeah." It was true. "I was behind the door and they didn't see me. They think I've changed."

Affa sat down and ran her fingers through my hair. All she needed to do was go a little lower and untie me, then I'd be free.

"You've changed?" she asked.

"Not really. I don't think so... Or maybe I have just a little or a WHOLE LOT." It was time to tell Affa the truth, the whole truth and nothing but the truth. "Well, I guess it all started with the food fight, the day we lost our family honour." And then, everything spilled out of my mouth: Bashir spreading lies, becoming Form Captain, the posters, Mustafa getting into trouble, the Masked Trickster and the rest of it. I didn't know if Affa was going to get angry or worse, be disappointed, but at least I could finally tell someone who'd understand.

"So, I think I can win," I finished. "But it sort of feels like cheating… BUT I don't think I have a choice. How else will Amma and Nanu get back their honour?"

"Arrr God, Yusuf," Affa rolled her eyes and tried to squeeze the life out of me with a hug. "Who on earth told you that honour was about what people think of you?"

"Wait," I lifted my hands so she could untie me. "It's not?"

She laughed and began loosening my knots. "Honour is about who YOU are and what YOU do, not what people say about you. It's about doing the right thing, Yusuf, and if it doesn't feel right in your gut, then maybe something's wrong in here." She pointed towards my chest. "And I know my little brother – he is the man of this house after all." She gave me a hug. "I don't think he's a cheater, do you?"

CHAPTER FORTY-FOUR

"We have to stop the prank at all costs," I told Mustafa at school the next morning. Election Day was finally here: the banners were up, the whole class was buzzing, and the butterflies inside me had evolved into giant man-eating wasps.

"Say no more, Spider-Bhai," he said, shaking his head. "I have a plan."

"You do?" I stopped in my tracks on the way to my chair. "How did you know I'd call the whole thing off?"

"I didn't." Mustafa pulled his chair out and slumped into it, trying not to draw attention to himself. It was a good move because Sairah was spying on us. Even though she said she was on our side, we still couldn't trust her. "But my mum said that if you cheat, we can't be friends anymore, so it was either call off the prank or take you out - for the greater good obviously." He pulled out a skipping rope, a mini glue gun and a tin-opener from his pockets. "I guess I don't need these anymore."

I gulped, plonking into my chair too and shaking the

creeps off me. There was no time for that. "So, what's the plan, Batman?"

"We have to either tell a grown-up that we've made contact with the trickster and drop ourselves in it or..." Mustafa paused, as Miss Minchell rolled onto her chair. It was only a matter of time until she asked us to be quiet.

"Or?" I asked, fearing the worst.

He paused for a heartbeat. "Or you're the second speaker and—"

"And the prank is on me," I finished, watching Miss reach for the register and clap her hands for silence.

"Okay everyone," she called, raising her arms. "Settle down, settle down. Today's the big day."

Suddenly, a heavy hush descended over the class.

Miss Minchell rose from her seat and pointed one hand towards Bashir and the other towards me. "Today we'll see who has the honour of being Form Captain."

GULP.

"So, who wants to go first?" she asked, smiling at us both.

Bashir's hand shot up. I glanced at Mustafa, who was nodding slightly. With a heart that was trying to bust out of my ribcage, and the deepest breath I had ever taken, I kept my hand firmly down.

CHAPTER FORTY-FIVE

If you had asked me what Bashir said in his speech, I absolutely would NOT be able to tell you, because even though my body was there, my soul was somewhere else. I saw his lips move, I saw everyone clap when he finished, and I watched him bounce his way back to his seat. But, all that time, my ears had forgotten how to do their job and everything played in slow-motion on mute, until Miss Minchell said, "EARTH TO YUSUF? YOO HOOO, ANYONE HOME?"

"ARGH!" I squealed, almost FALLING OFF MY CHAIR! Whoever had kicked me was about to feel my... my...

But suddenly, the room felt alive again. All eyes were on me and a fire began raging over my cheeks.

"I said it's time for our second speaker." Miss paused and, for a second, I thought I saw the shadow of the Joker pass through her face. "Are you feeling okay, Yusuf?" she asked, looking at the others as if they could explain the CHAOS in my brain. "There's a fresh bottle of water on the front desk if you need it."

He was here. The Masked Trickster was here. I could feel it in my bones.

"Earth to Yusuf?" she asked again.

I should just say I'm not okay, right? I should just say that I felt sick, that lumps of gloop from last night's meal were clawing their way up my throat and would explode at any time. Affa's chicken curry would soar like fireworks towards the ceiling, before a pepper particle shot clean into Saleem's nostrils and a lone potato knocked Liam clean out. Saying I was sick, even though it was a lie, was definitely the right thing to do. I could just say that, right?

"Ummmmmmmm, well now that you mention it..." I began, trying to calculate my next words.

In the corner, Sairah was scribbling away and started whispering something to Saleem. Bashir was sniggering with Liam and Mustafa had his hands up in du'a.

Oh maaaaaan. I couldn't just give up now. If I wasn't the second speaker, then Miss Minchell would be. I mean, who else would announce the winner?

I was left with no choice but to scope out the front of the room where Miss had placed the microphone she had borrowed from Music.

It was decision time.

Looking Miss Minchell in the eye, I stood up tall and

puffed out my chest just like the Falcon did, like the Winter Soldier did and exactly like those who came before them. After all, not all superheroes wore capes. Some of them wore school uniforms (like me, Spider-bhai).

I took a DEEEEEEP breath and pushed my chair in.

"I'm ready," I said confidently. Then I whispered 'bismillah', praying for some miracle to stop the disaster I was walking into.

CHAPTER FORTY-SIX

"Is this thing on?" I tapped the microphone from the front of the classroom, but instead of saying yes, the thing **SHRIEKED** LIKE IT WAS ALIVE! "Make it stop! Make it stop!" I shouted, trying my best to hold onto it.

"MAKE IT STOP, MAKE IT STOP!' the microphone echoed in the squeakiest voice.

WAIT! That wasn't my voice! Why did it sound like I had swallowed a hot air balloon full of helium? And WHY WAS EVERYBODY LAUGHING?

"It wasn't me!" I squeaked.

"IT WASN'T ME!" echoed the microphone, in a pitch that only dogs could hear.

Miss Minchell rolled forwards in her chair, but who knew what the trickster had planned? I pushed the microphone away from me and took a step back. "No! I'm okay. You stay there!" I waved my hands to show her how serious I was. I had to stop her from getting too close!

Miss raised an eyebrow and turned to the rest of the class. Saleem had disappeared into the neck of his jumper (he was shaking so much with laughter), Mustafa had his eyes closed again (but had now moved onto putting his hands over his ears as well) and Bashir was holding up a paper with 'You da best' written on it (but when Miss looked away, he unfolded the little flap that revealed the word 'LOSER!').

Focus, Yusuf. Focus. Let's just get this over with.

"As-salamu 'alaikum everyone, greetings earthlings and good morning 5B." Great start! Now, continue. I shook my head and took another breath. "My name is Yusuf Ali Fan."

Bashir guffawed and the rest of the class copied him.

Oh man.

"Ahem, my name is Yusuf Ali Khan, and you may know me as the boy who has been wrongly accused of attacking the local Imam, but I'm here to prove me wrong – I mean 'you' wrong, not me! You!"

Right, what was next? I pressed rewind in my brain and tried to remember what Affa had told me to say. Something about honour and good character and being a leader when people needed it most.

I glanced at Mustafa, who lifted a shaky thumbs up and pointed towards the bottle on the teacher desk.

Good idea. It would buy me more time while I thought of what to say next.

With all eyes on me, I reached for the bottle and pressed hard to take a sip ONLY FOR THE WATER TO SQUIRT ALL OVER ME! It slapped me in the face with a huge SPLAT, missing my glasses and shooting itself directly into my eyes.

"MY EYES! MY PRECIOUS EYES!" I hissed over the laughter. "Miss, it burns us! It burns." But the pranks weren't finished.

OH NO! THEY WEREN'T FINISHED!

"I'M OKAY!" I yelled back. "I'M OKAY! STAY EXACTLY WHERE YOU ARE!"

I stretched my arms out to find my bearings, but it was hard with all the noise. Between the howling and the sniggering from all corners of the classroom, I didn't know my left from right! Blindly, I ran forward, but SMACKED straight into a door handle, before boing-ing straight onto the carpet.

"Oh my God!" OH GREAT, now she calls God! SHE HAD ALL THIS TIME! But wait, why did she sound so far away? And why was everyone clapping?

I tried to drag myself up with the coats on the pegs, but a backpack launched itself at me instead, missing my nose by mere centimetres and knocking my glasses sideways. A shower of cheese strings, burst Whotsits and sandwiches innards rained all over my face, threatening to drown me. I didn't want to eat it, but my tongue had a life of its own!

SPLAT!

I fixed my glasses only to find a Peperami spear wedged into my armpit and a ham slice above my heart.

"NOOOOOOOOOOOOO!" I had already had enough piggy drama to last me a lifetime! Throwing the ham slice into the air, I rolled back onto my feet and finally got my balance. But all the laughter had gone and an eerie silence followed.

Slowly, I turned around… to see Miss Minchell's face had disappeared behind a pale slice of buttered ham.

CHAPTER FORTY-SEVEN

Mr Boayke had the whole of Year 5 and Year 6 in the hall, while Miss Minchell 'blew some steam' in the staffroom. Because the Year 3s had just had P.E., the benches were still in rows and Mr Boayke gave us permission to sit on our future thrones. Since I knew I wasn't going to win, at least I got this as a special treat.

"Right, everyone settle down," he called above the chatter. It was like we were in a football stadium, and everything felt electric. "I hear some of us have had a bit of an eventful morning."

A huge super-giggle ripped through the room; even the Year 6s had been tickled. It was no secret that news at Western always travelled at the speed of light, with or without Sairah's help.

"While the votes for Year 5 are being counted by Miss Minchell," Mr Boayke took his seat next to the piano. "I've decided to get you together to share the importance of democracy."

It was now Mr Boayke's turn to get on the microphone

(not that he needed one – you'd be able to hear him over a stampede of wooly mammoths if he had the chance). "Listen carefully, everyone," he began without a single squeak. "Today you've had a taste of what it takes to decide your leader…"

Mr Boakye's voice trailed off into the background, as Aadam snuck his way towards me and Mustafa. We activated spy mode and shuffled quietly to clear an opening for him. Sometimes, it was hard not to believe that his secret superpower was shape-shifting into a scaredy-cat.

"Yusuf!" he whispered. "I can't believe you took the fall. What about your honour? Mum told me that Affa's here. Don't tell me she persuaded you. WHY DOES SHE ALWAYS RUIN MY PLANS FOR WORLD DOMINATION?"

Mustafa shook his head and pushed a finger to Aadam's lips. Boakye was onto us. The mighty eye of democracy hovered over us again. Aadam snapped his lips shut. Even though he was 136 days older than me, sometimes I felt like maybe I was beginning to be a wiser egg than he was.

I double-checked to see if any eyes were on us before answering.

"I don't want to win like that, Aadam. Ever." I whispered, but straight away Mr Boakye locked onto me again. When you have to choose between picking a bogey and a fight with Mr Boakye, I think we all know which one is the safest option. I quickly stuck a finger in my nose to cover myself. "Plus, Affa said that the first step to being a good leader is making sure that people vote for the real you. I don't know who 'me' is yet, but it's not a cheater. Who even wants to be Form Captain anyway? Right, Mustafa?"

But Mustafa had stopped listening to us. He had been frozen to the spot in Mr Boakye's trance.

"Mustafa?" I repeated. "Mustafa?"

But nothing.

It was like he had zombied out. Not Mustafa. Anybody but Mustafa. Take Aadam instead, yaa Rabb, but leave my Mustafa alone. "Come back!" I whispered.

Aadam prodded me in the ear without saying a single word.

Something was wrong. I could feel it… behind me.

A shadow loomed over us like it was preparing to pounce. A shiver ran down my spine and my spidey-senses were tingling.

It was the Masked Trickster. It had to be.

Breathe, Yusuf. Breathe.

It's not going to hurt you. Not in front of all these people. No way.

I took another deep breath.

But the thing behind me must have done the same because I COULD FEEL IT BREATHING ON MY NECK!

IT WAS THE MASKED TRICKSTER COMING FOR VENGEANCE! IT HAD TO BE!

"DUN DUN DUN!"

My heart lunged into my throat, just as Mr Boakye lifted his fingers from the piano keys.

CHAPTER FORTY-EIGHT

A wave of silence followed. Everything moved in slow motion, and it was like we were underwater. The whole hall was facing the front and it was obvious that the only person who detected the presence of the trickster was the one who was foolish enough to summon him. (Yep – that was me.)

Just turn around, Yusuf. Just turn around.

You can do it. After three. Just do it.

I took another deep breath.

I could do it, right? No Masked Trickster is going to make a fool of Yusuf Ali Khan.

Okay, okay.

LET'S DO THIS, SPIDER-BHAI! GAME ON!

One.

But what happens if it launches itself at me and takes my eyeballs out? I needed those to see!

Two.

But I still hadn't finished growing! I had so much left to smell!

Three!

I whipped myself around only to see that MISS MINCHELL had eaten the Masked Trickster WHOLE!

"SAY IT'S NOT SO!" I shrieked, pulling on the ends of Miss' dress. "WHY OH WHY OH WHY? I DON'T DESERVE THIS!"

All of a sudden, all eyes were on me, and a ring of fire raged through my cheeks. I closed my eyes, feeling the weight of everyone's stares. They were going to laugh at me. It was ONLY A MATTER OF TIME! Where was the hole that I needed to crawl into?

I shook my head.

This wasn't happening.

Not my cool points. DON'T HURT MY COOL POINTS! They were the only shreds of respect I had left.

I closed my eyes tighter, as Miss tugged onto her dress. My next trick would be to disappear forever, right? RIGHT? There'd be a sinkhole that would take me to Nanu, and I'd wake up and the WORST DAY of MY ENTIRE LIFE (except for the day Amma posted my PlayStation to Bangladesh, of course) would be over. RIGHT?!

"O masked one of the tricking kind!" I called, squeezing my eyes firmly shut. "I mean, YA RABB, make it stop! Make it stop!"

And then the unexpected hit me like HUMONGOUS THUNDERCLAPS. Everyone in our class, and the Year 6s too, were stamping their feet and throwing their hands into the air. All of a sudden, I felt like I was flying as a trillion octopus arms tried to strangle me hands came to high-five me.

"Leave me alone," I squeaked as my body was raised into the air. I could see the light!

"I can't believe you did it, Yusuf!" Aadam squealed, getting to me first. "See, I told you my plan would work! Honesty is the best policy!"

"SAVE ME, MUSTAFA," I screamed, ignoring the gibberish falling out of Aadam's mouth.

"You got your honour back," Mustafa shouted, shaking my shoulders.

Wait, what?

Before I could think another thought, about ten billion sweaty 5B bodies swept me completely off my feet.

CHAPTER FORTY-NINE

On the Day of Judgement, when Allah azza wa jal asks me what I want in heaven, I'm going to tell Him that it's this moment.

In case you missed it, let me rewind and tell you ALL about the time I became FORM CAPTAIN of 5B...

REWIND

"Is this thing on?" I tapped the microphone, as it said my words after me.

We were all in the hall and my eyes had finally stopped sweating (sometimes I get hayfever in autumn too). Miss Minchell (the BEST teacher ever), Mr Boayke (the COOLEST teacher ever) and everyone else (the BEST MINIONS a leader could ever ask for) were all looking at me like the humble superhero I was.

"As-salamu 'alaikum wa rahmatullahi wa barakathu my dear brothers and sisters of Western Primary." It was

finally time to tell them what Affa had told me to say all along. "I just want to say a ginormous thank you to you all. Even you Bashir, even you. I couldn't have done this without you."

What? It was true! I owed him everything. Thanks to him, I had my honour back, and I couldn't help but pray that God gave him the same one day (yeah, I know I'd regret it later).

Instead of smiling with all his heart, Bashir stuck his tongue out. But because I was already on Cloud 29, nothing could put a bogey on my mood. No, sir. Nothing at all.

I scanned the hall. Mustafa gave me a thumbs up, Sairah was scribbling away as usual, and Saleem was making du'a (in shaa Allah for me).

"Anyway, I don't know what I did for you to trust me to lead you, but I want to make two things clear," I cleared my throat too to be on the safe side. "The first thing is that I will try my very best to be the leader 5B deserves and make this world a better place. I can't make any promises because I'm too scared of breaking them, but I just want you to know that you made the right choice, and I will not let you down. Thank you for helping me find my honour again." I gripped onto the microphone tightly. The next bit was the most important bit. Never did I ever think I'd hold so much power to make change for the better. But here I was, exactly the way that God had planned it.

"Secondly, I didn't eat any sausages and taking the Imam out with a chocolate cupcake was an accident, I promise."

There, I had said it. Everything that I needed to say was now out for the world to hear. It was my truth, and nobody could change that, not even Sairah.

Everyone cheered, as I made my way to the bench where Mustafa had saved my seat. Mr Boakye and Miss Minchell even nipped into the staffroom to get us some halal Haribos to celebrate.

"Here," Sairah passed me the freshest copy of The 5B Times. It was still warm at the bottom.

"Spider-Bhai Strikes Again!" Mustafa read, smiling from ear to ear. "Yes! You did it!"

"Cooooooooool" Aadam squeaked, reading the story.

But even though the headline was AMAZING, nothing prepared me for what happened next.

Sairah sighed and shook her head. "I just want to say sorry. For everything. I didn't mean to ruin things. I let the power of what I wrote go to my head. I should have told the truth, Yusuf. That's what a good journalist does. Truth over lies, right?"

THE
5B TIMES

SPIDER-BHAI STRIKES AGAIN!

_____

_____

_____

_____

_____

_____

_____

A huge **THUMP** cracked over the chatter, as Mustafa, Saleem and Aadam fake-passed out onto the floor.

"Did we just hear, right?" Aadam whispered, rubbing his head. "I think I'm dreaming."

"Nah, bro," Mustafa said. "We're dead and this is the afterlife where anything can happen."

But Saleem looked seriously worried. There were deep lines above his eyebrows. "Who are you and what have you done with my sister? She doesn't say sorry to no-one!"

Sairah shook her head again and took the newspaper back. "Can you forgive me?" she asked, twitching her nose.

This would be my first honourable decision as Form Captain.

"Always."

Her eyes jumped up and she smiled.

"Here," Mustafa said, getting to his feet. He threw us a khazoor each. "Let's celebrate!"

"You knew I'd win?!" He really was the best friend anyone could ask for.

"Not in a million years. I've just collected loads from mosque," he called over his shoulder. He sure could move fast when he wanted to. He passed one to Bashir too. "I don't really like them, but Mum would kill me if she found out I didn't. Here, Liam, have one."

Liam raised an eyebrow and inspected it carefully. "I thought you guys weren't allowed sausages?"

"No way!" Sairah shrieked, almost choking on her khazoor. "Are you kidding me?"

Bashir shook his head, and my jaw was so far on the floor that I was scared I'd trip over it.

"THIS IS A SAUSAGE? OH NO! THE MASKED TRICKSTER HAS STRUCK AGAIN!" Saleem yelped, nearly self-combusting. "Oh wait, no…" He triple, quadruple checked it. "It's a date. Phew!"

Aadam sniffed his one and then snorted, holding his tummy like it hurt. "It's medjool. It's like the nicest thing ever."

And he was right in every way.

This was definitely the nicest thing ever, and it was definitely a date to remember.

CHAPTER FIFTY

"Amma! Nanu!" I ran out onto the yard at the end of the school day, blasting my way like a shooting star. "You'd never guess what happened!" I squealed, trying not to smother them with ALL THE LOVE.

"You won Form Captain, baba," Amma said, smiling with every single one of her teeth and giving me the biggest squeeze ever. I didn't even care that there were witnesses.

"Yes!" I jumped onto Nanu and whacked straight into her. Nanu was as hard as nails.

"Beta, I see you've finally found what you've been looking for." She pinched my cheek, making it tingle.

"I don't know what you mean," I said, opening my bag to pass them both a khazoor each. "I had everything I needed right here."

Amma eyes grew into huge lamps, while Nanu snuck me a samosa that she had stashed inside her sari for safe-keeping.

I took a big **CHOMP** and waved goodbye to Mustafa as he ran to his car.

Everything was perfect.

Just perfect.

"You know what, baba?" Amma said, ruffling my hair. "It looks like we have two lovely surprises to celebrate today."

Surprise? What surprise?

Nanu caught the look on my face and smiled widely. "We'll let your affa break the news, beta. Things are going to be changing around here for good."

OH MAAAAAAAAAN! NOT AGAIN!

ACKNOWLEDGEMENTS

The story within these very pages is a love-letter to every brown reader out there, especially those who grow up feeling like they're the 'other', like they don't belong, and like they're the exception, not the norm. This one's for them. This truly would have meant the world to my younger self so I only hope that I've done it justice. I also know that being able to tell stories like this is both a blessing and a privilege, and it's certainly something I could not have done without the love, guidance and unwavering support of my Mama and Papa Bear. May He always grant you goodness.

To my sister, Gollum, thank you for every moment you've shared with Yusuf. As the dedication goes, this story wouldn't have been the same without you. I hope you know that I appreciate everything you've done for me. To my brother and my bhabi, thank you for being the continual, unspoken reminders to up my game and not settle for anything but the best version of myself. It's true what they say: our actions speak louder than words. To my not-so-little ladies,

Sairah and Hidayah, I hope you find yourselves in here one day.

To my aunties and uncles, my nieces and nephews, my cousins and close ones and more, thank you for the memories, the laughter, and those moments we'll hold onto when everything else falls apart and all we have left is each other. I'm so blessed to have you in my life. May He always keep us close.

To my agent, Polly Nolan, for starting the seeds of this series not so long ago. To my editor, Eishar Brar, how quickly time passes and these things wrap up – thank you for letting me be on this one. It was something I needed to prove to myself. To Marssaié and Farah Khandaker, thank you for bringing this to life so beautifully. To everyone on the Knights Of team, thank you for everything and more. I've done so many things that I wouldn't have dared dream of before, but somehow I'm here dreaming bigger.

To the staff and students at Lady Evelyn, alhamdullilah, I'm always grateful for your kindness, advice and du'a. Thank you for keeping me on my toes and helping me strive to be better.

And lastly to my nearest and dearest, thank you for everything, always.

BURHANA ISLAM

Author

Born in Bangladesh, raised in Newcastle and currently residing in the outskirts of Manchester, Burhana Islam is a storyteller who is passionate about exploring themes of heritage, belonging, identity and faith in her work. She studied English Literature at Newcastle University before deciding to become a secondary school teacher, sharing her love for stories with a new generation of curious, young minds. MAYHEM MISSION (2021) was her debut children's fiction book, and she is also the author of AMAZING MUSLIMS WHO CHANGED THE WORLD (Puffin, 2020).

FARAH KHANDAKER

Illustrator

Farah Khandaker is an illustrator and designer currently based in Dhaka, Bangladesh. She received her masters with distinction from Nottingham Trent University specialising in Illustration. She's worked across children's books, logos and editorial. Her work is fun and engaging with vibrant colour schemes and unique characters.

KNIGHTS OF

KNIGHTS OF is a multi award-winning inclusive publisher focused on bringing underrepresented voices to the forefront of commercial children's publishing. With a team led by women of colour, and an unwavering focus on their intended readership for each book, Knights Of works to engage with gatekeepers across the industry, including booksellers, teachers and librarians, and supports non-traditional community spaces with events, outreach, marketing and partnerships.